The Wondrous Tales of Ertah

Bob Roseberry

Ordering Information:

Dedication

This, my first volume of writings, is dedicated to my wife, Lisa (Ásil), who has put up with me through this whole ordeal. Besides her understanding for my need to undertake this project, she has been there with a needed synonym or two (more) when my memory or Google didn't suffice.

Table of Contents

Prologue

H ere are the tales that have been told over time by the great storytellers and sung by every bard that has ever sung a ballad in the world of Ertah. Stories of heroes and champions, evildoers and monsters, wonders and miracles - everything that makes a good tale enjoyable whenever told and retold. Prepare to be amazed, amused, awed, elated, frightened, sickened, a veritable magic carpet ride of emotions.

I, Veras of Asamel, have spent my lifetime collecting and collating these chronicles for the future enjoyment of all in Ertah. Many hours have I consumed reading manuscripts and documents from the libraries at Idon and Al Cene. Likewise, I have listened to every tale spinner and troubadour to cross my path in all these many years.

My wish is that you, too, will enjoy these tales enough to continue in their retelling for many years to come. So, sit back, get comfortable in a well-lit space, have food and drink at the ready, but, most of all, delight in. . . .

The Wondrous Tales of Ertah

The Wurm Queen

"From this point on, be as quiet as a slug," whispered the man. He, and his female companion, were attempting something that was punishable by death. They crept along the wharf searching for a viable place to secrete themselves for a long boat ride to Pellopus. The two had made this trip many times in the past as passengers. This time was different. This time they must not be found out.

The male, Rolo, and his partner, Amalah, were trying to break free from a life working on the slug farms. At first, "slugging," as it was called, was a tolerable vocation. Rolo had worked hard to get the promotion to "carrier." Amalah still worked in the yards harvesting the crawlers. As secure as they were in their lives, the slug farm was not a place to raise a child. Amalah was expecting.

The farming of slugs had become a lucrative business over the years. Slug "meat" was said to be a delicacy among members of the establishment. Only the best taverns and eating houses offer it on their bill of fares. To mask its actual pedigree, it has become known as gormat. Everyone is aware of the origin, but it sounds more palatable to say one is having a plate of gormat, instead of a plate of slugs.

The eating of slugs was only its secondary motivation for cultivation. Slugs produce "hru," an addictive narcotic used throughout Ertah by apothecaries, clerics, and doctors for medicinal purposes. Others use it for unethical reasons. These people are called "sluggers" because they are hooked on the "slug drug."

Through no fault of their own, Rolo and Amalah, were cursed with the dependency. Occupational hazard you might say. They were aware of the dangers and took precautions, but nevertheless, they had succumbed. A good reason, they thought, to escape.

Rolo's job as a carrier was to transport the drug to Pellopus where it would be distributed to legitimate customers. The job was perfectly legal inasmuch as he made the proper transactions. Where the drug ended up from there was not his concern.

This time he was not under the auspices of the slug farm. If apprehended, the punishment was life ending. He and Amalah could stow away in the hold of that day's launch then slip off the boat just before reaching Pellopus. All should go well.

The plan would have worked, too, but for a bit of bad luck. They had made it off the vessel and on to the shore without mishap a few miles from the city. Appearing as ordinary folk, which they were, they entered Pellopus looking to get lost in the hustle and bustle of the thriving mercantile town.

First, a room in a seedy inn was procured using their meager savings. With the success of the plan, better lodgings would soon be had. Amalah should "wait here" for the return of her mate.

Rolo had made a few business contacts in Pellopus on which he thought he could rely. This is where his plan starts to fall apart. The half-orc contact was intrigued by Rolo's getaway tale. Rolo purposely left out the part about a having a partner with child. What interested the half-orc most was the contents of the package which Rolo had brought with him from the farm.

For the last several official trips Rolo had made for the farm, he had slipped an infinitesimal amount of hru into his pockets. He knew from his dealings that the small quantity would never be missed. Over time, the collection became quite valuable. Now it was Rolo's time to collect his spoils.

The half-orc, seeing an opportunity, seized the package and ordered his men to make Rolo disappear. Alas, this is the last your storyteller has ever heard of poor Rolo.

Amalah, on the other hand, was left waiting for Rolo to return. As you can infer, she had a long wait. As squalid as the inn was, and it was, the proprietor was a businessman, and when no more rent was forthcoming, Amalah was obliged to leave.

On the streets, with child, destitute, and no job in the foreseeable future, Amalah's options were few. Begging seemed like a last-chance solution. Working at the slug farm was all she was trained to do, but that was out of the question, now. What was a young woman to do? Fortunately, until her belly starts to swell, she still had her looks.

And that, kind readers, is exactly what she did. Giving pleasure to men for money, it was not that big of a deal, and provided for her needs until the baby came.

It was a girl. She named her Auria. She had always liked the name. Auria Cara, Rolo's surname, became the terror of the streets of Pellopus. As soon as she was able to walk and talk, she made her "living" as a pickpocket and purse-snatcher. Because of her small size, and incredible quickness, she was somewhat of a pilfering savant.

Years passed rapidly. Her mother was never around anymore, so Auria had to raise herself. Some would call her a rowdy girl. There was not a boy around could best her in wrestling or fisticuffs. She could not remember ever taking a bath. Swimming naked in the river had sufficed. Her hair was infested, as were all the street urchins', so it mattered not. A mere ragamuffin of a child.

She had always been aware of her mother's ways and swore to never sink so low. What was the possible calling for a grownup street kid? Not that she was grown up. Always small for her age, which she could not recall, she had begun to notice some bodily changes that were mystifying.

Perhaps she needed a change of scenery. She had heard many bards' tales of adventures in her day. Maybe she had what it took to be an adventurer. Only one way to find out. Go on an adventure! She will never be missed.

The 5-day Festival at Riverport was nearing. Auria had always wanted to go to the annual festival celebrating the creation of the Tunnel between Riverport and Al Cene. Many ages ago, as the legend tells, the underpass had been dug by giant creatures called "wurm," thus, the Wurm Festival was initiated. "

"That would be perfect for a first adventure," she concluded.

When she was much younger and her mother was still around, her mother had told her the stories of her parents' escape from the slug farms by stowing away in a boat. If her mother could do it, it could not be too difficult. She had no belongings save for the clothes she wore and the knife she was never without. First rule of the streets, never be caught without a knife. She was ready for her first adventure.

A little jaunt down by the wharves, and she obtained the information she desired – the next boat to Riverport. Locating the vessel was not difficult. Now for the stowing away. Because of her innate skills of stealth, and her small size, this, too, was easily accomplished.

She pledged to herself to be attentive at all times, but the gentle rocking of the vessel caused her to enter into a much-needed slumber. With slumber comes the accompanying sounds that go with it. For such a small individual, Auria could snore inordinately loud. Her snorts gave away her presence. A sailor discovered the sleeping little stowaway and proceeded to arouse and upbraid the child.

"What's all the commotion, sailor?" A weather-beaten woman of indiscriminate age sauntered up.

"I have discovered a stowaway, Captain. Should I throw *it* overboard?" Auria did not care for being called an "it."

"You just try, mister," Auria warned.

"Brave words from such a small river rat, hey Captain?" the seaman taunted. He held Auria out at arm's length, the child violently swinging her fists to no avail.

"I must confess, she has spirit," admitted the crewman.

"That she does," acknowledged the mature female. "Settle down, girl. You are a girl, correct?"

"Of course, I am a girl?" Auria declared.

"Then, start acting like one," commanded the commander. At that, Auria calmed and became more civil.

"What's your name, girl?

"Auria."

"Pretty name," the captain acknowledged. "So, Auria, explain yourself."

"I am going on an adventure to the Riverport Festival."

"I see. And you were hoping to get a free ride on The River Maiden?" asked the old mariner.

"The who?

"Not who, girl, what," the old woman corrected. "The River Maiden is the name of my ship."

"Oh." Still confused. "That was supposed to be part of the adventure."

"I think I understand now, child. But what about your parents, will they not be concerned?"

"I have no parents that I know of. My father disappeared when I was a baby. My mother, well, just say I have lost track of her."

"Such a sad story from such a young child."

"I am not so young as you think. I am just small for my age."

"It is difficult to see when you are covered in so much grime. When was the last time you bathed, child?" No response. "What? Never? We will put an end to that!"

The captain picked Auria up and holding the child out in front of her, carried the wriggling girl into her private quarters. "She may be old," Auria thought, "but her hands are like steel." She was forced to strip and put into a metal tub and made to wait until some water could be warmed. The water was then poured over the child's head. "Hey!" she shouted. Something called "soap" was used to scrub every inch of Auria's body, especially behind the ears. The caustic suds stung Auria's eyes, making her cry. The captain could be very assertive and took no sassing from the youngster.

"That will do for now. I fear it will take many more baths to repair the damage done by so many years of neglect. Here is a towel, girl, dry yourself."

She would never admit to it, but she felt better than she had ever felt. "So, this is what clean feels like," she told herself while wrapping the towel around her newly scrubbed body. "I could get used to this." Years of emotions were hard to keep down and came flooding out in quiet sobs.

"There, there, girl, or should I say young lady? Who could have known that under all that filth was blooming a young woman. And a pretty one, too." No one had ever told her she was pretty before.

"I am afraid I do not have the proper clothes for a blossoming beauty as yourself. Not much use for them out here on the river. Size will be a problem also. I used to be a wizard with a needle and thread. I must have some spare sailcloth around here. Until then, wear these." She handed Auria the tops and bottoms of a prior cabin boy's togs which hung loosely but would serve for the time being.

"You are too kind, Captain."

"Nonsense, and none of that Captain blather. My name is Hermesta, Hermesta Tallon. 'Hermie' to my closest acquaintances, of which I hope will include you. Say, you must be starving, I will rustle up some food stuffs while you get out of that wet towel and into some dry clothes.

Auria did as she was told. The cabin boy's clothes hid the womanly curves of her freshly cleaned body and made her look boyish instead, except for the obvious swell of her adolescent bosoms.

"Here you go, Missie. It is nothing fancy, but it is the best we have." Hermie handed Auria a plate with bread and cheese, and some sort of dried meat that chewed like leather but tasted rather good.

"You fill out that outfit reasonably well," Hermie commented. "Maybe too well," she had to admit on taking a second look. "I may have to keep you locked up in my quarters. If the crew gets a gander at you, I may have a mutiny on my hands." Auria blushed, a totally new and gratifying feeling for the girl. Auria could not imagine a better start to her adventure.

Hermie was reluctant to allow Auria out on deck. What seems like ages ago, because it was, Hermie could remember too well what it was like to have a fair maiden onboard. Believe it, or do not, but she was once that fair maiden. Her presence on a ship had made the crewmen forget their duties and commit all types of fooleries. This young girl would surely have the same results.

"I will fill up time fitting her for a proper dress for a young girl," the captain told herself. "She cannot be walking about on deck with pins and needles holding her together. That would be enough for half a day, maybe. Then what?" Suddenly, this voyage was looking to be much longer than usual.

There is an adage about putting makeup on a wild boar. The boar may look nicer, but you are still left with a wild boar. Hermie was remembering that saying while watching Auria wipe her nose with her arm and then wiping that arm on her pants. The girl may look feminine, but she still behaves like the street urchin she is. "I must teach her how to be a girl before we reach Riverport." And now, the voyage seemed much too short.

To allow Auria free reign of the decks, Hermie would first need to forewarn the crew of possible issues. She warned them to be wary of any flirtations on their parts that might lead to complications onboard.

"She is only just learning to be a girl. You do not want her to have a bad opinion of men at such an early stage of her education." The crewmen concurred.

For an old sea captain, Hermie was a competent seamstress. The dress, made from sailcloth, was quite becoming on the girl. There was now no confusion about her gender. Auria felt uneasy wearing such an outfit. It made her feel different somehow. Hermie also made her an undergarment for modesty's sake. Auria thought it unnecessary, but Hermie was insistent.

"A young lady would never think of going out without them," Hermie cautioned. And so began the lessons. How to sit properly, how to eat properly, how to walk properly, how to talk properly - there were many things to learn about being a girl. Because of her natural abilities, and because she desired it so, Auria quickly doffed her streetwise ways and donned a more genteel self-assurance. It was now time to introduce her to the crewmen.

"All hands, on deck," the first mate ordered. When all were assembled, Captain Hermesta Tallon strode forward in a very magisterial manner.

"Gentlemen," she had never called them that before, "I wish to present to you Miss Auria Cara." Auria had been hidden behind the captain's form until now. Embarrassed, another new and curious sensation, she slowly revealed herself to the crew. Immediate gasps and mumblings sprang forth from the crew.

"Silence!" the captain was resolute. "As commanded, you will be on your best behavior around Miss Cara. I have allowed her some privileges on decks to make her voyage less confining. You will continue with your duties as if she were not here. Any improprieties will be vigilantly dealt with by me. I am sure you understand what that means," she threatened. "Very well, continue as you were."

This was Auria's first test as a young lady. The captain discreetly kept watch to assess her pupil's achievement. Auria's first impulse was to run excitedly to the side of the ship and look over the side. She caught herself and methodically strolled portside. "Good girl," observed the captain.

"Careful, ma'am," it was the first mate, "you would not want to fall overboard." It was the sailor who had discovered her days ago. "The captain is a miracle worker, if you do not mind my saying." She did not. "They call me Tolly. If there is anything you should want while onboard, just ask for me."

"Thank you, Tolly." She was remembering their first encounter when he had called her an "it," and a "river rat." Funny how quickly things change. "Possibly you could show me around and teach me the workings of a boat." She was honestly curious, but the crewman's attention was oddly stimulating.

"Well, first you should know this is not a boat, it is a ship."

"Sorry, Tolly, tell me more." And so, he did. The better part of the day was spent instructing her on the correct terminology and operations of the "boat." Always under the watchful eye of Captain Tallon, who was sure the first mate was above board in his actions. Auria had passed her first test with flying colors. "Nary a misstep," proclaimed Hermie. "You are on your way to becoming a proper young woman."

On retiring, Auria told Hermie, "Your first mate, Tolly, is a nice man."

"Yes, he is," admitted the captain. "Don't get any ideas there, girl. He is much too old for you." "Thank goodness we will drop anchor in Riverport tomorrow," Hermie told herself.

"The real test for you is fast approaching, the festival in Riverport." Auria had almost forgotten about the goal of her adventure. She would now have sweet dreams if her excitement allowed her to sleep at all.

The day was sunny, the ship was moored, all that was left was to disembark. Ensuring Auria's safety. Captain Tallon escorted the overly excited girl along the avenues of the seaport town. Not dissimilar to Pellopus, Riverport was teeming with possibilities. Auria had to restrain her instinctive impulses to acquire a purse or two. She was consciously trying to be a "good girl."

The festival, usually a 5-day affair, being the fourth year of the sun cycle, had a sixth day, called Wurmsday. This was the fourth year, so the carnival spirit was increased.

Actually, the festival was not officially on for a few more days. The town was preoccupied with preparations, which included the selection of the Wurm Queen. Any girl, 16 years of age, or older, could compete for the honor. Hermie thought this the perfect way to introduce Auria to the world and suggested it to her.

"Me," questioned Auria, "a queen?"

"Why not? You are a girl, are you not? And if there is any question of your age, I will vouch for you. My word has much weight in these parts. I have not been sailing these waters for these many years for nothing. Besides, you already have one vote, mine," Hermie confirmed. "That is correct, child, I am one of the judges."

The captain had been thinking of this since she had seen the transformation of guttersnipe into butterfly. If Hermie had her way, and she usually did, Auria would be crowned Wurm Queen tomorrow night.

Auria could not believe it. From street urchin to the possibility of becoming a queen in a week's time. How could her adventure get any more exciting? That, dear friends, is my mission to reveal.

The night of the Queen's Pageant had arrived. Auria was enthralled by the spectacle of it all.

"Oh, Hermie, I am so excited. To think that a street rat, could even imagine being a queen."

"Hush girl, we do not want the other judges to know your circumstances. Observe your competition, a collection of the spoiled issue of Riverport. I recognize some from pageants past. They enter every year until they either win or grow too old to be considered. I think your chances are favorable." Auria beamed.

Perhaps it was this inner glow, or, as Hermie had mentioned, her sway on the proceedings, or maybe it was just meant to be, but when all was done, Auria was chosen. "She had never looked prettier," Hermie thought. First mate, Tolly, a tag-along, could not agree more.

The queen and her matron were oblivious to the mumblings and jealous complaints of the losing contestants. The coddled losers felt cheated out of what, they thought, was rightfully theirs. Who was this little stranger, anyhow? The resentful also-rans plotted to do something about this terrible insult.

Upon her selection, Auria was paraded through town with all the pomp befitting actual royalty. Auria's adventure was coming to a marvelous conclusion, or so she thought. Unbeknownst to Auria, or anyone else, for that matter, she was being scrutinized by a spy of Ifn Adee, the sultan of Al Cene.

The spy was sent to Riverport to inspect the pageant winner as a possible mate for the sultan's son, Prince Ifn Parse. The prince was becoming a man and needed a bride to solidify his place in the dynasty. For generations the cities of Al Cene and Riverport had utilized the wedding bed as a way of keeping the Tunnel flowing freely between the two cities. It was now Al Cene's turn to make this happen.

Locating the girl was uncomplicated for she could be found at several functions in Riverport by the fanfares that preceded her. As Queen, she was expected to reign over the festivities on this, the first day of the celebrations. The spy must needs follow her around until an opportune time presented itself. He noticed the girl was always accompanied by an older woman. Too old for a mother, a grandmother, maybe?

The sultan's man finally found that opportunity and introduced himself to the older woman.

"If you please, madam," he said with a flourish. "May I present myself to you and your companion."

"Go ahead," the captain said full of suspicion at this oily-looking man.

"I am Afnash D'Brini, adjutant to His Highness, Ifn Adee, the Sultan of Al Cene. I have been sent as his advocate to invite you and your companion to the royal palace in Al Cene. This is merely another benefit of being chosen the fairest of the fair. The sultan wishes to meet the Queen and give tribute in person."

Auria was dumbfounded. Not only was she a queen, but a sultan wished to "give tribute" to her. "Will wonders never cease." She could barely catch her breath.

Hermie wanted to give Auria the adventure of a lifetime. This sounded promising.

"All of the arrangements have been made. Travel, there and back, accommodations and a feast in her honor, are all included." Not wanting to scare them away, he left out the part about the betrothal. "Let her meet the prince first," he thought, "maybe she will surprise everyone and like the boy."

They made arrangements to meet the following morning next to The River Maiden. Before that, some shopping was in order

"You cannot expect to be presented to a sultan wearing a dress of sailcloth," Hermie avowed. "You will need appropriate traveling apparel in addition to a fashionable dress for the feast."

"A feast," Auria bragged, "in *my* honor."

"Control yourself, dear," Hermie chided. "Do not let all of this go to your head. Remember, this is but for one week, then what? You have your whole life ahead of you to think about. Have you even thought of what you will do when this is all over?"

Auria was sobered by the thought. "She had no trade skills," she admitted to herself. "Picking pockets and purse snatching were all she knew." She refused to return to that life. Maybe she could be a cabin girl on The River Maiden, spending her life sailing back and forth from Pellopus to Riverport. She and Tolly would marry and settle down and raise a family. When Hermie retired, Tolly would become captain of The River Maiden, and. . . .oh! who was she fooling? "I am dreaming," she told herself.

The shopping spree was as enjoyable for the captain as for Auria. The girl could spend the rest of her days trying on clothes. This was the most fun she could ever remember. At last, they decided on the suitable clothing for the trip ahead and made their way back to The River Maiden.

Auria told Tolly all about her day, especially the part of the sultan's invitation.

"I am to be feasted by a sultan. Me!"

"Well, the river rat has come a long way," mocked the seaman, feeling a little jealous.

"Maybe they will have gormat. If they do, I will save you one." The word made her think of her mother who had mentioned the delicacy once in a conversation.

"More likely they will serve you eels wrapped in grape leaves," Tolly joked. "I have heard they crave those in Al Cene." It was fun bantering with Tolly.

Auria was up all night imaging the next day, until exhaustion finally gave her sleep.

"The sultan's carriage awaits," announced the adjutant the next morning. Hermie and Auria had been up early making ready for the trip. Auria, in her new travel attire, could not wait to get on the road.

"Just think, Hermie, we are going to be riding through the Tunnel." This would be a new experience for the captain as well, who was dizzy with expectation.

"Thank you, Auria, for including me in your adventure."

Riding in a horse-drawn carriage was another new experience for Auria. The sultan's transport was of the highest quality with so much room she could lay out and take a nap. Of course, she would then miss the awe of moving through the Tunnel.

She could not even imagine the size of the beasts that first burrowed underground and under the sea to create this wonder of Ertah. Some say they were the ancestors of the slugs her parents used to raise. "Could it be possible?" she wondered.

Hermie, too, welcomed the bit of pampering they received as guests of the sultan. She did not remember any of the past queens being treated so royally. The captain suspected other motives for this treatment, but did not want to bring it up to Auria and ruin her special day. The captain would be watchful.

All good things must end and so, too, the junket through the Tunnel. The sultan's palace was but a short distance from the egress and they arrived far in advance of the feast.

The two guests of honor were shown to their quarters where they could rest until the festivities commenced. Two canopied beds, with netting for protection from flying insects, had been placed in the room for their use. A small table containing plates of food was provided. On one plate, Auria observed some gormat. Upon sampling, it was not to her liking. Possibly, it brought to mind unpleasant memories. Be that as it may, she wrapped one in a cloth and pocketed it as promised to Tolly.

"My parents once worked on the slug farms. I suppose one might say that is where my life's journey began."

"Now is not the time to dwell on the past," Hermie said. "We must get you ready for the meal in your honor. Now, slip out of those clothes, and put on your new dress. You want to look your best when meeting a sultan."

Hermie wished for a way to preserve this moment. Auria was beyond beautiful in her fancy new dress. The captain was thankful her first mate was not present. Even Tolly, usually a man of honor, would lose control.

The adjutant, Afnash, arrived to escort Auria and the captain to the banquet. "The queen is looking lovely tonight." Coming from his mouth, this compliment sounded sinister.

"Thank you," was all Auria could think to say. The remainder of the promenade was in complete silence.

The feast was held in a large open-air room. Guests were seated on pillows in a circle around the space. The sultan's place was plain to see, as he, and another individual, prince Ifn Parse, as Auria would soon discover, had the only table and chairs in the room. The adjutant ushered the guests of honor in front of the ruler.

"Ladies, may I have the honor of introducing to you His Royal Highness, Ifn Adee, Sultan of Al Cene. Your Highness, Miss Auria Cara, Queen of the Wurm Festival, and her consort, Captain HermestaTallon of The River Maiden."

"My pleasure, ladies. And might I introduce you to Prince Ifn Parse, my son and heir to the throne." The prince was maybe twelve years old and quite affected.

"Father, is she the one?" asked the prince. "If so, I approve."

"Later, boy, now is not the time."

Auria was disquieted. "The 'one' for what?" she wondered.

She and Hermie were shown to their seats. The feast was begun. Attendants entered with platters heaped high with meats, fruits, vegetables, breads, every sort of food a person could want, even gormat. The sultan lacked nothing and wanted his guests to know.

Wine flowed without end, it seemed. Hermie kept a tight watch on Auria to see she did not lose control. The captain allowed Auria a few sips of the liquid, out of respect to their host, but requested something less intoxicating for the remainder of the meal.

When the feasting neared its end, the sultan arose and raised his goblet high.

"A tribute to the lasting accord of Al Cene and Riverport. May the contract of our two municipalities be honored for all time." All were in assent.

"To that end, I would like to propose the requisite union between our fine city-states. My son, the heir prince of Al Cene, has chosen Riverport's Wurm Queen, Auria Cara, for his bride. What say you all?" Loud huzzahs could be heard around the room.

"What just happened?" Auria asked Hermie.

"I think the sultan has just announced your betrothal to the prince. This is preposterous," declared the captain.

"Do I not get any say in this?"

"Of course, you have a say. Let me handle this."

Hermie stood, and in her loudest river captain's voice cried out, "Attention, please!" The room became still. "There seems to be some confusion. Of course, Auria is honored to be considered for the position, but do you not think you are taking things a bit hastily? The two have barely just met. Maybe some time for getting acquainted is called for?"

"As you will," the sultan conceded. "The boy tends to be a bit impulsive when he sees something he wants."

"Auria was not a plaything for the prince's dalliances," thought Hermie. She must get Auria out of this situation as politically as possible. The sultan was, after all, providing for their means of transportation back to Riverport.

"Your stay in Al Cene shall be extended for as long as it takes the two children to become more familiar. Shall we say a week?" A week on Ertah lasted six days.

"Sir, as you know, I am a river tradesman. As so, I am needed to sail my ship from Riverport to Pellopus. Many others are reliant on me for their livelihoods. Would that I had six days to give you, they would surely be yours."

"I completely understand, captain. Your transport back to Riverport will be provided, as promised. You may be assured the girl will be safe here. As I understand things, the girl is an orphan and you, ma'am, are merely an acquaintance and have no familial ties to her. Correct?"

"Well, yes, that is how it is."

"The spy has done his job well," thought Hermie. The sultan appeared to have an answer for everything.

"We are finished here, I think," the sultan ended, and left.

Back in their room, Auria and Hermie discussed the recent state of affairs.

"He is but a boy," Auria professed, "and a not very pleasant one, at that."

"Silence, Auria," warned the captain, "you do not want to be overheard."

"Betrothed to a silly boy is not how I expected my adventure to come to an end."

"Nor I," Hermie complied. "Try to get some sleep, girl. Tomorrow promises to be a day of decisions."

Believe me, or not, but the two were able to finally fall asleep, and a sound sleep it was. Neither was disturbed by the band of thugs who entered their quarters, quickly gagged Auria, and absconded with the girl.

Who were these kidnappers and why take off with Auria, you might ask? I will tell you. They were a group of brigands, led by one Razooli. They had been hired by the father of one of the overindulged runners-up who had had some dealings with the self-entitled Warden of Ul. His instructions were to abduct the girl from the palace and extract her from the Al Cene-Riverport area for good. No questions asked.

They were paid well for their crime and carried out the misdoing without a hitch. Well, almost. They did misplace the girl. One night she was there, the next morning she had disappeared. By then, they were so far into Ul, they assumed the girl had escaped and was lost in the desert, the meal for some desert creature, mayhaps.

What of Captain Tallon? Well, the following morning, upon discovering the offense, she, with the sultan's aid, conducted a search to no avail. She reluctantly returned to her ship and crew. Her final days were consumed by the memories of a little street rat that just wanted to have an adventure.

And there, kind readers, is the tale of the Wurm Queen. Some stories have happy endings, others, sad to say, the opposite. That is the way of Ertah. ---So be it.

My next tale, dear reader, is the bizarre story of . . . .

The Beast from the Forgotten Isle

∽

The drums could be heard from a long distance away, also the chanting. The village was in preparation for the Ceremony of Courage. The candidates had reached the approved age and were making ready for the night's activities to commence. Each had already received their markings signifying their coming of age. The marks needed to be applied a year in advance of the ceremony to completely heal, and for the recipient to recover.

Aranac, son of the late Bardac, had chosen a shark tooth and spearhead design that intertwined covering his entire right shoulder and down his arm. The body art had taken months to complete and was extremely painful, even for someone as large as Aranac.

Most Arandarian males were much bigger than the average males of Ertah. It was not unusual for a male from the Forgotten Isle to be over 20 king's hands in height, the standard of measurement being the width of the reigning king's hand. Though rulers come and go, it has been found the hand width is almost the same from king to king. The present king, Boolac's, was no exception.

The women of Arandar were, strangely, the antithesis of their male counterparts. Normal sized for Ertah, 16 king's hands on average, fair to the eye, they were the embodiment of the female. Arandarian coupling can only be left to one's imagination.

For an Arandarian, Aranac was considered huge. At nearly 24 king's hands, he towered over his fellow aspirants, and was therefore considered somewhat of a freak of nature, but in a good way. He had always been the biggest boy of his age group and able to perform amazing feats of strength.

In spite of his size and strength, Aranac's mother, Moolac, sister of the king, raised a good boy. He would never harm anyone or anything unless provoked. Then, watch out. His rage was the talk of the village. Even King Boolac feared upsetting the boy.

When Aranac got into one of his moods, the only thing that would calm him were the words of Princess Amarac, King Boolac's daughter and Aranac's cousin. She knew just the right words to say, and how to say them, to tame the beast in the boy. They had known each other since birth and had grown fond of one another over the years. Amarac wished only the best for her cousin's chances.

Each stage of the event should be child's play for the brute. After the initial chanting and dancing concluded, the celebrants would be taken to the Cursed Jungle to spend the night on their own. Aranac's father had lost his life in the same jungle on a hunting excursion several moons ago.

If they survived the night, some would not, the following morning they needed to proceed to the Pongac Cliffs, where they would attempt to scale the treacherous 300-king's hands high rock-face to the top, where they would then dive into shark infested waters. The initiation was complete when the warrior returned to the village with a shark's tooth, the evidence of their manhood.

All children of Arandar are acquainted with the scary stories of the Cursed Jungle. Around the fires at night these frightening tales would be told and retold to teach them, from an early age, to shun the dangerous place. Some did not heed the warnings. Some suffered the consequences.

One spear and one knife were all each candidate was allowed. Naturally, if I forgot to mention, they were completely naked except for a band around the waist to hold the knife. Each warrior-to-be needed to get as much sleep as possible to better accomplish the following day's tasks. Lack of slumber had been the main reason for many candidates to fail the energy-sapping climb and subsequent shark battle.

Aranac was unconcerned with the foretold fears of the jungle. He had complete confidence in his abilities. It was the climbing and diving that bothered him most. The rocks were slippery, and he did not care for swimming. He made himself a bed of fronds and leaves and fell to sleep with these worries to nag his dreams.

He had just made the dive, in his dreams, when a massive shark grabbed his leg and started to pull him down. He kicked at the creature with his free foot in vain. His lungs were about to burst when he awoke to find a giant snake wrapping itself around his leg.

The future warrior acted quickly. He grabbed the snake by its neck turning the tables on the hapless reptile. The constrictor was now the constricted. Aranac squeezed with all his might until the serpent went limp. He hung the body on a branch above his bedding to warn off any other animals that had similar ideas of ruining his rest.

His totem worked and he was well-rested for the remaining day's feats. Others were not so lucky. Some could not last the full night and quit the campaign. Not every man was meant to be a warrior. Some were never heard from again, sacrifices to the jungle. Or there were runaways, too, embarrassed to bring shame on their parents. Best the villagers believe they, too, were an offering to the dreaded place.

Aranac, and the remaining few contestants began the trek to the cliffs. Jogging the whole distance, never needing a respite, he reached the precipice ahead of the others and immediately set about his ascent.

Leaving his spear behind, he cautiously scaled the wet bluff. The day was quite windy which effected his climb. A couple of times he felt his grasp on the rocks give out, which would have meant the end of his trials. It was at these times he would think of Amarac to bolster his drive. He would be too ashamed to face her if he failed.

At last, he was atop the summit. All that was left was to leap into the waters below, kill one of the waiting sharks, remove a tooth, and return victoriously to the village. Simple. Not for you or I, dear reader, but we are not like Aranac.

With knife in hand, the behemoth of a man drew a large breath, held his nose with his free hand, ran, and jumped. On the way down, he had just enough time to think of Amarac, awaiting his return, before he plunged into the water. There were no sharks to be seen. His enormous splash had scared the fish away. He treaded water until they returned.

At first, they swam slowly around him, wary of such a large figure. Before one could choose him for a meal, Aranac chose the closest and slammed his knife into its eye. Blood poured forth, causing a frenzy amongst the remaining sharks.

These sharks did not know the meaning of the word frenzy until Aranac displayed his rage. He began slashing at every shark who neared him. When all was said and done, Aranac was the only creature left alive. "I will leave these here for the other warriors to find," he thought.

He swam to shore pulling the shark behind him. He made his way back to the village, extracted tooth in hand, the symbol of his manhood which he would wear proudly until his dying breath.

Amarac was the first to congratulate him. She would have hugged him, but their size difference made that awkward. Her face is adjacent to his male parts, and he was still naked.

The following day, no longer naked, wearing his customary breechcloth, he was set to receive the finishing touches on his shoulder art that would mark his completion of the warrior status. A circular space had been left unmarked on the middle of his upper arm to imprint the moon sign design of the village warrior. Hating to see her cousin in pain, nonetheless, Amarac was proud for Aranac's accomplishment.

As reward for their achievement, each new warrior was granted the available woman of their choosing as a mate. First to finish the ordeal received first choice, and so on. Amarac had dreamed of this moment for many years. Of course, Aranac made Amarac his choice. When Boolac was made aware of this, out of jealousy towards the warrior, he forbade it.

Boolac had always kept an eye on Aranac since his size and strength became evident. In their tribe, the most fit male was always chosen as king. Boolac was fearful that Aranac would one day vie for kingship. And now he wanted his daughter, also? Had Boolac known that Aranac would never have thought of usurping his uncle's power, maybe what happened next could have been avoided.

Before the two could make their wishes come to pass, the king sent his daughter to one of the Three Sisters Islands off the northwestern tip of the main island. These islands had been set aside as the harems for the king's wives, one island for each wife. It was forbidden for a male, even the king, to set foot there.

These harems were protected by troops of female warriors, bred for the positions. Trained from birth, enlistment in the troops brought honor to the family. Their mastery of the martial arts was renowned and a deterrent to any would-be male with second thoughts of breaching the prohibition.

Aranac was no would-be male. His longing for Amarac led him to make a rash decision. On a moonless night, the warrior set sail in a raft of his own construction to rescue his fair maiden. Not knowing to which isle she was taken made the task more problematic.

Aranac's size was also a problem. It is hard to sneak around when you are so large. Plus, the king had apprised the female warriors to be watchful in case the man attempted such a thing. Add to that the blow darts tipped with venom from a jungle treefrog and you have the makings of a real disaster.

He was doomed before he had a chance. At the first island he set foot on the women warriors were waiting and he was dead in the water, almost. The poisoned darts only slowed him down. His rage attack was lessoned to the point that it only took several female warriors to pin him down and bind him.

Continual use of the treefrog venom kept the brute under containment. King Boolac announced immediate banishment from the island. But first, a facial mark of dishonor to brand him for life as an outcast. This mark was the most painful of all. Not because of the physical agony, which was excruciating, but for the shame he brought upon his mother.

With his face swollen and unrecognizable as a human, Aranac was set adrift in the same self-made craft he used to get in this predicament, with only his knife at his waist and his shark tooth hanging from a cord around his neck.

Aranac floated aimlessly for days. He came to think he was the only one left in the world. His attempts to acquire food were fruitless. The fish were too quick and any bird he saw was too distant to capture. Any thought of returning to the Forgotten Isle was rebuffed by the scars on his face. Any other tribe on the island would know what those marks meant.

Ertah's oceans are dotted with islands, atolls, archipelagoes and dormant, and not-so-dormant, volcano tops poking out of the water. The probability that Aranac would discover land was on his side. After days of meandering the disgraced warrior came upon one such land mass protruding right up in front of his raft.

The smallish haven of sand, trees, grasses, and various other plants seemed habitable. The evidence of crabs and other shell life would help fill his empty insides. As far as he could tell, he was its only resident.

His first consideration was fresh water. He had been subsisting on periodic handfuls of sea water to stay alive. Although he had been cautioned of doing so since early childhood, a man has to do what a man has to do.

Dry of mouth and light-headed, Aranac searched for a spring but came up empty handed. Some large-leafed plants had traces of moisture left behind from a recent rainstorm. Aranac, animal-like, lapped the water off the leaves. His warrior training informed him to make bowls from these leaves to catch fresh water from future rainfalls.

Next on the agenda was food. He had seen crabs walking sideways down the sands when he landed. The crustaceans happened to be Aranac's favorite seafood. He had been catching and eating them since he was a youth.

Crabmeat alone was not enough to suffice such a huge person. His early education in the ways of the warrior had taught him survival skills for just such an occasion. If there were birds on the island, it would be logical there must be eggs to be found. Fishing would be difficult without a net. He could fashion a spear to impale them. It looks like our hero will have to get used to swimming.

Lastly, a shelter was called for. As much as Aranac welcomed a good shower, he did not want to be out in the rain all day and night. With bamboo and fronds readily accessible, the warrior built a fine safeguard from the elements.

Days turned into weeks. Aranac had become quite adept at staying alive. Storms were quite frequent, so fresh water was not an issue. There was no end to crabs, and he had become very proficient with the spear he had made. Schools of fish were prevalent amongst the coral reefs that surrounded Amarac, the name he gave to his new home.

One day, while exploring on Amarac, he came upon something odd. A land fowl that could not have flown here on its own. The little islet would not have any animal life not introduced by man. Until now, Aranac had seen no signs of humans having ever been there. Curious.

If anyone had been present to watch, they would have been amused by the giant's attempts to capture the hen. Yes, my friend, she was tending to her eggs when our hero interrupted her reverie. Bending and stooping while trying and not succeeding, to catch the fowl was hilarious. He abandoned the venture until the next day when he would return with a basket to ensnare the mother hen.

Aranac named his pet hen Clac. She laid eggs almost every day. Besides nutrition, Clac gave the lonely Aranac much needed companionship.

While crabbing one day, Aranac looked to the sea and saw a sail. His first response was to attract attention, but he thought better of it. His face, almost fully healed, would still frighten the boldest of men. He would hide in the trees and wait to see what was to transpire.

The ship anchored offshore and a small rowboat with three men oared to the beach. Once ashore, they disembarked and scanned the shoreline. Aranac was unfamiliar with other men of Ertah. They seemed weak and pale in comparison.

"This looks a likely place," the man with the large scar across his face said, only Aranac did not understand the noises he made with his mouth.

"Yes, sir, captain, as you will," another man replied.

The three men then attempted to raise something out of the rowboat, a box that was apparently too heavy for the three to lift. Aranac, always looking to lend a helping hand to others, his mother raised him well, left his hiding place and approached the struggling sailors. Their reactions were to be expected.

"Captain, what is it?" screamed one of the men. They pushed the boat back into the water to escape, but the warrior was too quick. Aranac grabbed the stern of the rowboat and dragged it back onshore.

By this time the men were frantic. One drew a weapon made from a shiny substance Aranac had never seen. When the man used the weapon on Aranac's arm it caused him to bleed. That was enough for the beast to emerge. He picked up each man, one at a time, and threw them back in the water.

Next, Aranac pulled the boat, with its load, up the beach toward his shelter. "This is a much finer vessel than the one I came on," he thought.

He picked up the box with one hand and attempted to open it with the other. The men, now out of the water, stood and watched in horror and amazement.

"Sir, have you ever imagined such strength?" one seaman uttered.

"No, sailor, I have not. Do our eyes deceive us? Or perhaps we have been to sea too long," the captain reckoned.

Unable to open the box, the Arandarian tossed it aside as if it were nothing and continued up the beach. He now picked the boat up and carried it above his head. The seamen just stood dumbfounded.

"How will we return to the ship without our boat?" asked one awestruck sailor.

"Do you suppose it can speak, captain?" implored the other.

"Let us approach him and find out," replied the commander. "Be on your guard, men."

The captain and his two mates yelled to get Aranac's attention. The man-beast stopped, turned, and placed the boat back on the sand. He could not understand their rantings.

"Aranac," said Aranac, pounding his chest with his right fist.

"Come again," the captain asked.

"Aranac," the warrior repeated with the same hand gesture.

"Are-a-knock," said the captain.

"I think that is its name, sir," said the shorter of the two crew mates.

"Captain Pataman," announced the officer, pounding his fist on his chest.

"Cap'n Pah-tah-mahn" Aranac's mispronunciation coming near enough for the captain.

"Yes, yes," the captain declared, thinking he was making progress, "that is sufficient."

The captain had a wild idea. Using hand gestures, he motioned for Aranac to pick up the box and carry it over his head to a secluded spot in the trees. Aranac did so without breaking a sweat. Next, he motioned for him to dig a hole like an animal would. Aranac obliged, squatting down like a dog, and throwing handfuls of dirt to the wind. Finally, the captain mimed putting the box into the hole and burying it. The task was no trouble for Aranac.

"This beast could come in handy," the captain quipped. "I propose we take him with us."

Burying treasure was not the only duty the captain had for Aranac. The "beast," as the crew would come to call him, could also be valuable in any future skirmishes. His size and grotesque countenance would scare the fiercest of challengers.

Getting Aranac to accompany them was a bit of an issue. First, they needed to convince the beast to come with them. Through gesture and mime, they conveyed the idea of going with them to the ship. But every time they were sure he understood, Aranac would walk away. Finally, they realized he wanted to get something. He left and came back a few minutes later holding a spear and a chicken. Now, he was ready to go.

The transfer to the ship also caused some concern. The rowboat was not big enough for the four of them. It was decided to make two trips. The captain and first mate would go first to prepare the rest of the crew for the beast. They would send another sailor back to collect Aranac and the remaining crew member.

Aranac sat on the deck of the boat where the treasure had been. Clac sat comfortably on his lap. The two sailors sat beside each other, rowing. The new crewman was agape for the entire return trip.

Once onboard, Aranac was introduced to the rest of the crew.

"Mates, this is Are-a-knock, our new crewman," the captain announced. "He seems tame enough, but do not vex him for fear of your life. As you might guess, he is quite powerful." As a demonstration, the captain mimed for Aranac to raise the mainsail. What usually required several seamen to accomplish, Aranac did alone. He grabbed the rope and pulled the main sail to its full height. The crewmen were not only astounded they were pleased that such a helpmate had joined their number. And for that, Aranac became as a pet to the men.

Speaking of pets, some crew members had been looking at Clac thinking it would be good to have boiled chicken for dinner. But the captain's words had stuck – "Do not vex the beast, or, else." Clac was off limits to the crew.

The following days were happy ones for Aranac. He enjoyed showing off his strength for his new friends. If there was a job nobody wanted to do, "Let the beast do it," became a familiar maxim around The Black Scorpion, the ship's moniker.

The captain did not mind. His crew had not been this cheery since their last big freebooting. You see, dear reader, if you had not reasoned, The Black Scorpion was one of the most feared pirate vessels in the southern, or any other, sea. Captain "Scarface" Pataman and his crew had prices on their heads.

His first inklings that something was amiss was when they spotted another ship sailing in their waters. The Black Scorpion was built for speed. She, the ship, would be adjacent a prospective quarry before the other ship could maneuver an escape.

At first, Aranac thought it was some sort of game. His crewmates swung from ropes to land on the neighboring vessel. It looked like fun, so he joined in. At the sight of him, the other ship's crew were so terrified they surrendered immediately.

Aranac's mates would gather up the crew from the neighboring ship and, using planks, walk them over to The Black Scorpion. Some chose to jump for their lives rather than being captured. You see, they were going to end up as slaves. Slavery was a big business in this part of Ertah. Alas, my friend, were it not so.

Once onboard The Black Scorpion, the seized crew were chained and placed in the hold of the ship. There they would remain until a slave market could be reached, like the one at Boleole. There, they would be sold to work in the gem-filled mines in the mountains of the island of Lansit.

After looting the ship for anything of value they set it on fire. Aranac could not understand why his "friends" were being so unkind to the other ship and its crew. It did not seem right to the kindhearted beast.

Two more days and two more sacked ships later, with a full hold of human merchandise, The Black Scorpion was primed to make landfall. Aranac remained onboard The Black Scorpion both times and let his crewmates do the dirty work.

Boleole, pronounced Bo-lay-o-lay, his mates told him, was a seaport on the western coast of Lansit, an island south of Carfia. The island was divided into east and west by a range of mountains. These mountains were well known for their resources. Besides the aforementioned gems, emeralds and rubies especially, plentiful deposits of gold had also been found.

These riches were not going to just appear out of thin air. Workers were needed to extract them from the earth. Nobody in their right mind would want to do that kind of strenuous, backbreaking work, so, slaves were required.

That is where Pataman and his mates made their biggest profits. Besides capturing ships on the high seas, they would apprehend villagers up and down the coast of Carfia. That was Pataman's main rationale for "rescuing" Aranac in the first place. He knew a beast the size of the Arandarian would bring a hefty price at market.

Boleole was drawing nearer. Pataman needed a way to shackle the beast. His main concern was the creatures burst of rage. How was he to discover if iron chains would control him?

Aranac loved to play games that showed off his strength. "Let us test his powers," thought the captain.

First, the captain had him display his ability to lift heavy objects. Nothing was too weighty for Aranac. Tasks that required more than one seaman to perform, such as raising and lowering the sails, was easily executed by the Arandarian.

"Let us see if you can break loose from these bonds," Scarface asked.

These manacles and chains were made of the same material as the weapon the captain had used on their first meeting. It had cut Aranac and made him bleed. He avoided this material whenever possible. But for this game, Aranac would consent.

Using almost all his power, he could not break loose. Aranac did not like this material. A tug-of-war between Aranac and the rest of the crew was next. The outcome was a stalemate until the captain pulled out his whip and lashed the beast.

"Why you do that?" wondered the beast. "This game is not fun anymore."

"Heave men," the captain cried. "Throw him in the hold with the others."

"There is no room, sir," replied the first mate.

"Make room, sailor," the captain ordered.

Saddened, Aranac gave up the fight and was crammed into the hold with the other chattel. His hold-mates, still frightened of the beast, shied away from him as best they could.

The slave market was situated conveniently close to the wharf where The Black Scorpion was moored. The human commodities, shackled together, were marched onto a small stage for observation.

No stage was needed for the beast as he stood king's hands above everyone else. The usual crowd at these auctions was not at a loss for words. The murmuring and haggling began at the sight of the beast. Captain Pataman rubbed his hands in anticipation. The captain could never have anticipated what happened next.

Aranac had had time to plan for his escape while sitting quietly in the hold. He was overcoming his fear of the shiny material, "eye-ern" his fellow hold-mates had called it. The crew of The Black Scorpion would all come ashore for the auction. They all had a share in the outcome. If he could escape and be the first back to the ship, he could easily raise the main sail and be off.

The only thing hampering his plan was the eye-ern stuff. He grabbed the handcuffs and strained with all his might. He felt his rage coming on. It was now or never.

Aranac broke free from the manacles but was still fettered to a whole line of men by leg irons. When Aranac moves, everyone is obliged to move with him. He jumped off the stage and made a mad dash for The Black Scorpion. Those hapless folks chained to the beast had no choice but to run with him or be dragged behind.

As hoped, he and his "followers" were the first to reach The Black Scorpion. He quickly unmoored the ship, turned her seaward with a shove of his hand, jumped on board, raised the main sail, then stood with his new crew and fought off Pataman and his mates until the ship was on its way.

As I have said before, The Black Scorpion was built to sail faster than other ships. By the time Pataman was able to scrounge up another vessel and get all hands on deck, the deck of The Black Scorpion was long gone.

Aranac's new crewmates, all seasoned sailors, had no problem taking up where they had left off. The Black Scorpion was in able hands, and they did not mind when Aranac joined in. How soon fear of something becomes unconcern when you have like goals.

The crew all agreed the ship's name had to be changed. The Black Scorpion became The Intrepid. It made no difference to Aranac for he knew not what any of the names meant. His grasp of the common language was improving, though. He understood more than he spoke, which was not often. With the aid of gestures, he was able to make himself understood.

"What we do now?" he had asked when they were safely out of harm's reach.

"Hey, what do you know," one crewman quipped, "it can speak."

"Aranac speak good," the beast uttered.

"So, you can," the crewman agreed. "Well, I think we should select someone as captain just to keep things moving smoothly."

"Aranac pick you."

"Thank you, but it needs to be a majority. Does anyone object?" No one did. They did not want the responsibility that went with being captain. So, crewman Julian Flagg became Captain Julian Flagg of The Intrepid. And, to answer Aranac's initial question, Captain Flagg gave the order to bear north and set sail for Salé.

Aranac had missed his pet, Clac, since being placed in the hold. He was afraid she might have wound up on somebody's dinner plate. He searched and searched until he came upon her inside a coiled rope that looked like a nest. Indeed, she had employed it as such for it was filled with eggs. United once again, Aranac and his fowl friend awaited landfall.

Salé was a town on the western coast of Carfia, just south of the Rimalampa mountains, the highest in all of Ertah. Some of the crewmen from that area unsuccessfully attempted to teach Aranac about snow. The concept of freezing was beyond his grasp. Many concepts of Ertah were still unfamiliar to the young Arandarian, he had much to learn.

The city of Salé was nothing more than some wharfs for mooring ships, structures where the city folk dwelled, and an inn with a tavern, The Icy Sow, known for one thing – cold drinks. You see, the tavern owner, a dwarf by the name of Gladrik Redfall hired men to fetch wagonloads of ice from the nearby mountains. Gladrik had mined these mountains for years. He had always wanted to own a tavern. He had the idea to bring ice from the mountains to the lowlands. The Icy Sow was the culmination.

Aranac drew stares wherever he went. Salé was no different. When he entered The Icy Sow the patrons of the tavern stopped whatever they were doing with one collective gasp. Some stood in a panic preparing to flee.

"Avast all!" shouted Captain Flagg. "He is not dangerous. He is just large, that is all." When the patrons saw how Aranac cradled a chicken in his arms, they started to relax. He brought Clac to find her some proper chicken food.

"Cold drinks all around from the new captain of the ship Intrepid." Captain Flagg was relishing in the moment of his promotion. "An especially cold one for my friend here."

Aranac, almost dropping the drink because of the strange sensation it had on his fingers, gulped the ale down in one swallow.

"Aranac like," the big man pronounced. "More!" More was brought.

"What make drink feel this way?" Aranac wanted to know.

"Gladrik," the captain called. "Come and show our friend the magic."

The "magic" was a large block of ice. More plentiful than gold, the tavern owner had "struck gold" with his icy idea. Stored in a room full of straw, the ice was chipped with a chisel and the shavings were placed in drinks. It was also found that some foods, especially fruit, tasted better when chilled.

"Alas," moaned the tavern owner, "it is getting more difficult to acquire the stuff. Giant mountain creatures have been ambushing my transports leaving no one alive. Some men call them 'snow demons' and refuse to make the deliveries. Forsooth, I thought your large friend one of them when he stepped through the door, albeit a hairless one. He is the same size."

"Say," Gladrik sounded off. "Would your friend be looking for work?" The idea came in a flash. "I would pay him well to guard my deliveries to, and from, the mountains. He looks like he can take care of himself."

"Not only that," the captain agreed, "but he would make the work faster as he can lift the blocks of ice with no problem. He kind of enjoys showing off his strength."

"Good to hear," Gladrik said. "It is too late to start a haulage today but, first thing tomorrow."

Aranac and Clac spent the night in a shack. The man-beast fashioned a nest from straw for his pet. The hut reminded him of his home back in Arandar. He wondered how Amarac was doing.

"Arise friend," sang Gladrik waking the Arandarian before first light the next morning. "You will need to get an early start to reach the snow line. Here, I hope they fit." The dwarf handed Aranac a robe made from some animal furs and a pair of knee-high moccasins. "My woman had to guess at the measurements."

Believe or do not but the robe was too big. "Better to guess high than low," quipped the tavern owner. "How about those moccasins?" They were a bit snug but better than no shoes at all. Aranac was not so sure, having never worn foot coverings in his life.

Clac would be left behind for the short trip, safe in her nest. The robe was not needed until the weather deemed so. Aranac would carry it in a sack around his shoulder. It was recommended he wear the moccasins to "wear them in" so as not to get blisters.

The work team consisted of three other men who took turns driving the oxen-drawn cart. Aranac could ride in the cart on the way up but would need to walk on the return trip. Little was said between the men and Aranac for the entire outing. The three were a bit unnerved by the man-beast and Aranac preferred it that way.

The Arandarian was intrigued by the change in scenery as the journey progressed. First, were the unusual trees. They seemed to reach to the heavens, and had no leaves, just green needle-like growths that blanketed the "jungle."

As the group went higher, the tall trees gave way to a gray, rocky terrain. It was here the party decided to stop for the night. Camp was set up and food was given out. A chewy meat product not unlike the dried meat back home in Arandar. This, and cold water, chilled naturally. Aranac was prompted to don his new robe for the temperature was lowering rapidly.

The weather can change quickly in the mountainous regions. When Aranac made his bed of straw in the wagon it was merely cold. As the night drew on, a wind picked up, making it seem even colder. Aranac was grateful for the fur robe. He had never felt such stinging temperatures before.

He was awakened in the middle of the night by an unearthly howling. He knew the sounds were why he was here. Somehow, they sounded sad but comforting. They lulled him to sleep.

When Aranac awoke in the morning, the world had changed. It had snowed during the night leaving a white vista in all directions. The crewmen had tried to explain snow to him but seeing was believing. Like anyone who has never seen snow, Aranac danced around and shouted with joy in the white stuff like a young boy. The other three men, veterans of this ice run, just watched and shook their heads in disbelief.

The icefields were a short distance from the campsite. The glacial expanses provided unending supply for

Gladrik's taking. The three men chopped and sawed until a huge block was freed from the glacier. Now was Aranac's time to shine. He picked up the hunk of ice, heaved it over his head, then dropped the ice. Not because it was too heavy but, because the coldness burnt his fingers.

"I can not feel my fingers," Aranac shouted. The others laughed at his awakening awareness of numbness.

"Here, use these." One of the men handed him some gloves that were too small to wear regularly but held between the menacing ice and the skin of his hands, sufficed. Now he was able to exhibit his prowess by carrying the block of ice to the wagon with the full appreciation of his on-lookers.

Three more blocks were acquired using the same method. After a full day's labor, they were ready to return to camp. The mountain paths were dangerous by night, so it was decided to stay the night and make the return journey next morning.

With such decisions, my dear reader, are lives changed forever. By the time everyone ate and laid down to sleep, the wind had picked up steadily. The snow began to fall, a blizzard was eminent. Added to that was the same howling sounds from the night before, only this time they sounded closer.

Aranac, wrapped in his robe and sitting on a log, heard the screams first. Something was being slaughtered near him. He reasoned that the only animal that could scream such was a human. The only humans were the other three men. An arm fell next to him. He saw nothing else. The snow and wind had caused a blindness of a sort. Aranac could see no enemies to attack.

The enemies could not be seen because they were the color of the snow. The "snow demons" he was sent to defend against were having their way with the three ice cutters. Aranac stood, not knowing what to do, and then, all went black.

When he awoke, he found himself lying on the ground in what he assumed was a cave. A fire in the center of the cavern gave warmth and light. What he saw in this light was an assemblage of white furry creatures all about his size. One of the beasts noticed Aranac rousing and made the others aware.

The apparent leader of the tribe approached Aranac and grunted. Aranac, sitting up, grunted back. The group of creatures made sounds that Aranac guessed were sounds of laughter. The Arandarian stood, frightening some, at first. His robe fell to the ground. This brought a different reaction – wonder.

He quickly picked the robe off the ground and placed it around his shoulders. The demons all wanted to touch this amazing removable fur and stuck out their hands to feel it. The leader lifted one side of the robe to get a closer look at what was underneath. Aranac grabbed the garment away and recovered himself. That brought on more of the laughing sounds.

These creatures, Aranac thought, were not thinking animals, but clever, like the monkeys he had seen on Arandar. They had no real speech but could communicate with each other using grunts and squeals.

"Wait!" Aranac thought. He was confused. "If they do not think," he wondered, "where did they get fire?" Another thing he wondered was "Why am I still alive?" Without an obvious language his questions remained unanswered.

He could only guess that because of his size they mistook him as one of their own. That would answer the question of his present condition, but fire?

As he spent more time in the demons' camp it became clear. One demon was responsible for the upkeep of the fire. His job was to see that the fire never died out. Perhaps, out of curiosity, they had stolen the first flames from the camp of some past victims. Or maybe a tree was struck by lightning. However, they had it now.

Aranac's next question was, "How do I get out of here?" He did not even know where "here" was. "How far had they carried me away from the icefields? Will they just let me leave?" So many questions.

He did not have to wait long for his chance to escape. At night, the creatures would leave for their regular forays. They left Aranac by himself so the Arandarian took the opportunity slip away.

It was dark, there was no moon. He had only the stars to guide him. His warrior training was of no use, the astral signs were not the same at this region of Ertah as on Arandar. The only direction he was sure of, was down. So, down he went, being careful not to run into his demon friends.

For two sunrises and two sunsets the man-beast made his way down the mountains. His training kept him nourished by recognizing what plants were good or bad to eat. He did not arrive in the land of tall leafless trees. Instead, he discovered plants with sharp spikes. And sand, lots of sand. Sand as far as he could see. Nothing to do but start walking.

His robe was of no use now as the temperature had steadily risen on his descent. He still wore the moccasins that were made for him by Gladrik Redfall's woman. Aranac was grateful, as the footwear kept his feet protected from the burning sand.

Food and water were now an issue. He missed Clac and her fount of eggs. He hoped she was fairing well in his absence. She had done fine on the island before he discovered her so, for that, he was consoled. That did not solve his immediate problem.

He still had his knife, so he carefully cut into the spiky plants. They produced a liquid that made do for his lack of water. When de-spiked, he found them chewy but lacking in taste. Aranac, the warrior, could survive on less.

He decided north was the logical direction to go so, using the sun to guide him by day, he went that way. Now, good reader, had he decided to go east, he would have found an oasis just a few miles away. But that is a story for another time.

He continued north and stopped when he heard the familiar sounds of people in distress. What looked like a caravan of importance was being beset by a massive insect with a stinger on its curled-up tail.

Aranac, born to help the oppressed, went into action. Unafraid, the Arandarian ran, then jumped onto the big bug's back. Several knife stabs in the bug's body had little to no effect. He jumped down and grabbed the monster by a leg, attempting to flip it over, all the while trying to avoid that stinging tail.

The monstrosity finally lost its balance and rolled over. Aranac hopped onto its stomach and plunged his knife into where, he hoped, the creature's heart should be. The bug continued to twitch but showed no other signs of life. To make sure, Aranac unceremoniously hacked off its head.

The thankful survivors of the attack were confounded by their good fortune. As if sent by the gods, this strange-looking hulk saved their lives. They were as fearful of Aranac, at first, as they had been of the giant scorpion.

One boy in the group stood forward and addressed Aranac.

"Brave one, are you man or beast?"

"Some have called me 'beast,' but I am a man."

"Then, have you a name," asked the boy.

"Aranac."

"Well, Aranac, you have done a great thing today. You have saved a prince. I am Prince Ifn Parse, son of the Sultan of Al Cene. We were returning home from a hunting party when we were set upon by this creature. My father's adjutant was unable to protect us, but you did a marvelous job. Please, join us, and return to Al Cene where, I'm sure, my father will reward you handsomely."

Aranac liked the sound of that. He would gladly take some food and drink as reward. And so, Aranac found himself in the city of Al Cene, awaiting the next episode in his life's story.

If you like, dear readers, you can read more about our friend from Arandar, in the story Adventures in Ertah. Until then . . . .

My next story for your reading pleasure is . . . .

The Tale of the Favored Son

The prophetess Ásil scrutinized her charts and manuscripts, observed the stars and planets, conferred with the "old ones" and everything pointed to a "special" birth. Mylyn, wife of Lead Councilman, Derek Bin Alden, was with child and had asked her childhood friend, Ásil, to "look into" her child's well-being and possible future.

Ásil informed Mylyn that all portents were good. Not only good, but unique. "Your son," she had already predicted the gender, "will be a person of great favor. He will be celebrated throughout all Ertah."

These omens were a blessing to Mylyn. She had been deemed fallow, unable to bear children. She could not remember the last time she and Derek had coupled. It was taken to be a miracle birth by those in the know.

Derek became very suspicious of his wife, no matter how she pled ignorance of the enigma.

The birth itself was unexceptional. The child had all its fingers and toes and cried like a normal child would. If this was a "special" boy, he hid his "specialness" well. He played normal childhood games with average results. His schooling was normal, he had trouble with calculations and his manuscript was abysmal.

If there was one thing he excelled at, it was athletics. He could outrun any boy his age, and most older ones, too. He could jump higher, throw farther, and outwrestle all his peers. And, to his mother's disdain, out fight them in fisticuffs. Be that as it may, his physical capabilities were of no concern to his father.

The Domain of Alden, once a monarchy, was now under the control of the Council. Dirk's father was the leader of the council and he expected his son to follow in his footsteps. Nothing was further from the boy's mind. He could not bring it upon himself to tell his father this. He waited until he was of proper age and secretly joined the city-state's army. He explained himself to his mother but could not face his father's wrath.

The life of a soldier was the right fit for Dirk. Because of his athleticism he shined at every aspect of a soldier's being. He became the best at every weapon from sword to lance, longbow to sling, dagger to great axe. The other soldiers refused to spar with him for fear of injury. His life as a soldier missed only one thing – true combat.

He was bored for the want of a real fight. His father and the Council were good at what they did – diplomacy. Alden was not at war with anyone.

"What good are my skills if I never get to use them?" he wondered.

So, after saving his soldier's pay for several months, he deserted and headed west where things were said to be more unpredictable. He learned to appreciate the life of a loner. Soldiers were taught to fend for themselves, and at this too, Dirk excelled. He never lacked for food or drink. The life of an adventurer was one he valued.

In his sojourn west he observed towns and villages, each with their own salient points but, none interested Dirk as much as Pellopus.

Any young man on his own for the first time is liable to be faced with numerous temptations too irresistible to refuse even for one as strong-willed as Dirk. Wine, women, and wantonness were just waiting for the young soldier to arrive.

The first vice to take hold was drinking. Not only did it taste good, liquor made him feel good. Under the spell of alcohol, he thought himself stronger, braver, and more invincible. He was willing to take bigger risks.

Back home, he fancied himself a lady's man. He had his pick of the fair maidens of Alden not only for his talents and good looks but, because of his father's significance.

The women of Pellopus knew nothing of his former life. They only liked him when the money and alcohol were flowing. His soldier's savings were dissipating quickly which led him to the vice that corrupted the most – gambling.

Every kind of game of chance was prevalent in Pellopus. Lotto, cards, dice, wheel of fortune – they all were looking for fools and their money. Dirk tried his hand at all of them and found that he was not as lucky as he thought.

Down to his last copper, he bet 22, his age, on the wheel of fortune. The wheel stopped on 21. Out of money and luck, the young man was destitute. A deserter, a drunkard, a wastrel - he refused to go home and face his parents.

Dirk was in need of a job or some other way of acquiring money. He was a regular at one gambling den, The Favored Hero, that had a job board with local postings for services wanted. Dirk read one that sounded promising. 100 gold pieces were being offered to anyone brave and skilled enough to defeat a Boreal bear. Bravery and skills were two things at which Dirk excelled.

Dirk went to the address on the posting and met Grumbus Rurbag, a rich half-orc merchant. "I have always wanted a stuffed Boreal bear to decorate my retail outlet," he confessed. He was willing to pay big money for the artifact.

Dirk knew little of Boreal bears but was penniless and out of options. He guessed Boreal bears could be found near the Boreal Sea north of Pellopus. He was told the white-furred bears lived in the northern-most section of the sea which was ice-covered year-round.

After receiving an advance on his pay to buy supplies, Dirk could be quite charismatic when he wanted to be, he started his pursuit on foot, having recently lost his horse in a game of dice.

The trek was laborious, mostly uphill, and getting increasingly colder the further north he went. Always keeping to the shore of the great sea, the ice was finally reached.

Being white, the color of snow and ice, the bears would be hard to locate. It was the month of Frin, late winter in Iram, the bears would be living on the ice instead of land, adding to the difficulty. Ice was slippery.

The former soldier felt that surprise would be his biggest advantage. Little did he know, the Boreal bear had the most developed sense of smell of all Ertah's creatures. They would sense the human long before he could see them.

Fortunately for Dirk, Boreal bears are solitary beasts except for mother bears raising their young. He hoped for the former, nothing worse than a mother protecting her cubs to make your day disagreeable.

Dirk knew they were not going to come to him, and he could not wait them out to return to land so, he would have to go out on the ice to look for one. He did not have long to wait.

Maybe a mile onto the ice, Dirk saw a movement. Luckily for our hero the wind was in his favor blowing from the north. And there were no cubs in sight, a lone male.

Still too far for a shot from his longbow, Dirk inched ever closer. When he felt the time was right, he let loose an arrow at the beast. Dirk had never shot arrows in such a blustery wind before. The bolt passed by the bear and landed harmlessly in the snow. Dirk's surprise attack was foiled.

The Borealian bear, dear reader, is also one of Ertah's fastest land creatures, humans included. The bear, now aware of Dirk's presence, turned and made a mad dash at his tormentor. With no time to notch and shoot another arrow, and the footing too slippery to run, Dirk stood his ground and prepared for the fight of his life.

The bear was much bigger up close, nearly half as much taller than Dirk, who was a big boy. Dirk was feeling confident, though, claw and tooth against the steel of his longsword. What Dirk was not counting on was his lack of footing.

His boots were the finest made in all of Alden. Regrettably, they were not meant to be used on ice. With one mighty swing he fell right on his backside. Dirk had just enough time to regret every wrong in his life before the inevitable deathblow.

His mother's face was the last thing Dirk remembered before the impossible happened. With a loud "Whoop!" the bear was knocked completely off its paws by the strangest conveyance Dirk had seen to date. A triangular sled with a sail, being operated by an equally strange-looking man.

The confused animal was caught by surprise after all. That moment of discomfiture was enough for Dirk and his rescuer to finish the beast off.

"Much-obliged," Dirk declared.

"You would have done the same. No?" the stranger replied.

"But, of course," Dirk agreed, "but not in such a way. What do you call that thing?"

"No name, yet. I just recently invented it."

"I must say, your command of the Common language is outstanding," admitted Dirk as he inspected the leather-clad man.

"Not really, I have been speaking it from childhood." Dirk let that information sink in.

"I feel that is a story for another day," Dirk said. "I must now devise a way to transport this bear to Pellopus."

"I suggest you remove the bear from its fur first," the strange man counseled. "I could help."

The stranger was adept with his knife and had the bear skinned before Dirk could retrieve his spent arrow.

"Good job, friend. By the way, my name is Dirk, Dirk Bin Alden. And yours?"

"Kenbektoopali'Bevallimanawakasamsetra'zuman," pronounced the stranger. There was actually a click of the tongue at the end, kind reader, but I am unable to translate it into script.

"How about I just call you Ken from now on?" Dirk requested.

"As you wish," Ken agreed.

Ken fashioned two long poles from tree limbs into a sledge to carry the bear pelt. Both men, holding a pole end each, were able to drag the pelt to Pellopus and the waiting half-orc.

"Very good, sir. Here is your pay," Grumpus stated. "And try to hold on to it a bit longer. Less alcohol, fewer ladies, and stay away from those gambling establishments."

"Yes, sir. I have seen the error of my ways and profess to improve my life."

"Good to hear," Grumpus said, "and thank you again for my bear."

Back on the outside, Dirk split the money and tried to give half to Ken.

"This is the least I can do for your saving my life."

"I do not use money. I would prefer to travel with you in the future. I have the feeling great things happen around you. I wish to be present when they do."

So, just like that, Dirk and Ken were an inseparable duo.

The two returned to The Favored Hero, not to gamble or drink, but to check out the job board for any new postings. One posting got Dirk's attention:

Hero Wanted

The domain of Alden is in need of a hero. A hydra is plaguing our coast and villages. Many have died. Please, we beseech you to come to our aid. The Council is prepared to reward you handsomely upon proof of the monster's death.

My word is my bond, Derek Bin Alden

Seeing his father's name and woes caused Dirk to regret his past mistakes. He needed to return home and make amends. Ken agreed to accompany his new partner. But first, they required mounts and supplies. They acquired both, thanks to Grumpus' reward, and started off for Alden.

On the road, Dirk learned more about his new friend. Ken was from Iram, the land beyond The Thunder Mountains. His people were nomadic and had their "ways" with the land. Dirk was not certain what that meant, but it sounded good. The Common language was taught to him by a wise man from Oram who was studying his people.

Ken was curious about Oram and that is why he was on the ice the day he saved Dirk. The easiest passage through the mountains was from the north. After the mountains he was faced with the great frozen sea. When he discovered how slippery it was, he conceived of the idea to make a sled. Lacking dogs or any other animals to pull it, he devised a sail from skins of animals he had caught. The conveyance was working quite well until he ran it into a very large bear.

Dirk enjoyed the company of this clever Iramian. While making their way to Alden, they swapped stories, some true, others, not so much. Ken could tell a whopper with the best of them.

They came upon a forest that gave Ken a "feeling." He sensed something unusual, but wondrous about the place. Dirk thought it was a sign of the "ways" Ken had spoken of. The two entered the trees on full alert expecting something to happen.

Within moments of their entrance, they were surrounded by a squadron of graceful and cloaked, pointy-eared folk. Elves!

"What ho, strangers?" implored the biggest elf. He was not even as tall as Ken but demanded attention.

Dirk answered. "We are travelers intrigued by the unusual forest you seem to call home."

"Your kind is not welcome here. Please leave." Dirk did not take to being called a "kind" of anything and took offense.

"Sir," Dirk rejoined, "I assure you we mean you no harm. We were merely passing through on the way to my home in Alden."

At this announcement, the elves became disturbed. There was much whispering, in Elvish, Dirk assumed, for several moments.

"Alden, you say. And what might be your age?" the biggest elf inquired.

"I do not see why it matters, but I am 22 years of age." More Elvish whispering.

"If we have broken some law, then pardon our ignorance. We will return the way we came and seek another route."

"I am afraid it is too late for that," the elf stated. "You must come with us. Your friend is free to go." Now Dirk was really confused. "Why him, and not Ken?" he wondered. Grossly outnumbered, he had no choice but to surrender. Ken was forced to leave, but the well-trained and talented Iramian would always be nearby.

The elves, never taking their eyes off Dirk, led him deeper into the primeval woods. The scenery began to evolve around them from trees into arboreal structures of immense shapes and sizes, culminating with the largest, a throne room. Here Dirk was led and made to bow before the most beautiful creatures he had ever seen.

"Welcome, sir, to Lem," the beautiful male said, "last of the Elven strongholds. I am Isavar Ulakian, and this is my sister, Falerin Glynmer."

"I do not feel welcome, I feel as a prisoner would," Dirk remarked.

"Many apologies for any misunderstandings," the male elf said. "Certainly, you are not our prisoner. An honored guest, for sure."

"You have a funny way of treating a guest. I suppose the ways of the elves are unfamiliar to me." Dirk was using his charm to alleviate the situation. "So, why not let my companion accompany me?"

"What we are about to explain to you is not for all ears to hear. Our sentries sensed in you what we elves have been waiting for lo these many years. To better explain ourselves, I give you Ailwyn Sylvar, the chronicler of our realm."

A very ancient-looking elf stepped forward. Elves are known to live for hundreds of years, so Dirk guessed this one was as old as they got.

"It was foretold to us that a human-born hero, fair of face, would one day appear out of the east. This champion would be the protector of our world from all things evil. Uninterested in personal glory or wealth, this chosen one would be content with good deeds done."

"Our latest auguries, made some twenty years past, prophesied his imminent coming. We believe you to be that champion."

Dirk could not believe what he was hearing. "These people have been living in the woods too long," thought Dirk. "They believe me to be some kind of savior." Dirk was never privy to Ásil's prognostications.

"Well," he thought, "if it will get me out of here any sooner, I will play along."

Music from elven-made harps and lutes, with a light percussive beat on a drum, led off the ceremony. Pretty elven girls, Dirk wondered how old they were, danced gracefully all around. Isavar and Falerin marched in with the ends of their robes being held up behind them. Last in was the ancient elf, Ailwyn, the master of ceremonies. He began to speak.

"As was forecast in the stars many years past, a champion has come to us out of the east. Come, Dirk Bin Alden, kneel before me and prepare to take the Oath of Glory." Ailwyn motioned for Dirk to kneel. Dirk thought this was all too silly.

"Repeat after me (Dirk does so), I swear I will strive to be known for my good deeds alone. I will face hardships with courage and encourage my allies to do likewise. I will hone my body so its potential can be realized. I will marshal the discipline to overcome my failings that threaten to dim my glory and the glory of my friends. So be it."

While repeating the words, an otherworldly sensation overtook Dirk's body. Those that witnessed it would swear they saw an aura envelop his form. Dirk's mind was not his own. He was being spoken to by voices from long ago. When he awoke from his spell, Dirk was not himself.

He was ushered to Lem's eastern edge where Ken sat waiting.

"Ken, how did you know to meet me here?"

"I have seen it all from the tops of the trees. You were shining."

"Was I really? I do not remember."

"I believe a great thing has happened to you, as I predicted."

"I do feel different. It was an odd experience. Nevertheless, it is off to Alden we go."

Nothing else was mentioned about the curious doings at Lem. They rode diligently for two days and arrived at Alden near sundown.

Everyone was pleased to see Dirk. Everyone except his father. Dirk's past behavior had brought shame to the family name. His mother had been especially unsettled and had never been the same since his desertion. He went in search of his father.

"What do you have to say for yourself?"

"Father, I am truly regretful for the dishonor I have brought to you and mother. I promise you I am a new man."

"That may be so," the councilman remarked, "but rules must be followed. Guards! Please escort this deserter to the dungeon." Dirk was placed in irons and marched off to jail.

Ken, in the meantime, always content to be outside, made camp in the nearby woods. He would wait for word from his friend. The wait was longer than he expected.

Days went by, Dirk's only human contact was with his guard, Trebor, who would bring him leftovers from the kitchen.

"How long has it been?" asked Dirk.

"Let me see, you were brought in on Moonsday and it is now Fradensday. That would be," the guard used his fingers to count, "five days." He said it as though it was a great accomplishment.

"And no word from my mother?" Dirk was not even sure his mother knew of his return. "Could you possibly get word to her?" the prisoner asked.

"I cannot leave my post." The guard squished his face, trying to think of a solution. "I could maybe get my cousin to take her a note." That was a lot for the guard to think up. But Dirk liked the idea.

With a piece of trash paper and a crudely shaped piece of charcoal, Dirk wrote a short note informing his mother of his predicament.

It was not until the following Tinsday, that was three days later, that Dirk finally re-met his mother. At least, he thought it was her. She looked as though she had aged many more than the three years that had passed.

"Mother, I am so glad you have come. "

"Dirk? Dirk? Is it really you?" She even sounded like an old lady.

"Yes, Mother. I have returned to rid the realm of the dreaded Hydra."

"Ásil often reminded me that you were meant for great things. But do you really think you can do it?" Dirk, sadly, thought his mother was doddering.

"My friend Ken and I, I think you would like him, have been planning a strategy that, we hope, will do the job. He may be from savage lands, but he is quite clever when he needs to be. My only problem is this jail cell."

"I will talk to your father and see what can be done."

"Oh, and if I did not say it before, I love you, Mother."

"You always knew what to say to make your mother proud."

Two days later, on Thronsday, a dispatch of soldiers was sent to escort Dirk into his father's presence again.

"How are the accommodations? To your liking, I hope?" His father was enjoying this too much.

"Father, I am prepared to pay for my trespasses, but I have an idea to rid the realm of the Hydra. That is why I returned."

"You, boy? Be serious. What can you do, that others could not?"

"I have a plan. Actually, the plan is of my friend Ken's design. You see, father, the problem has always been the Hydra's heads. Each severed head always regrows, it is an unending dilemma. But what if the severed necks were to be seared shut, a new head could not grow. Do this enough times, and the Hydra will be destroyed."

"I see. But how will you sear the severed heads?"

"That is where my friend comes in. He is an Iramian of uncommon skills and intuition. As soon as I cut a head off, he will quickly follow behind with a torch and sear the wound shut. Teamwork will save the day."

"I must meet this friend of yours."

"He should be camped in the woods outside the castle. If you will, I will bring him to you."

Derek sent two soldiers to accompany his son to find Ken. The Iramian was relieved to see Dirk after such a long time.

"It has been a while since our last meeting," Ken observed.

"Let us say I have been otherwise occupied," Dirk admitted. "But I have good news. I have met with my father, and he is in accord with your plan. He wishes to meet the man responsible for it."

"It would be an honor to meet your father," Ken confessed.

They rode back to the castle where Ken was introduced to the Lead Council. Derek was immediately intrigued by Ken's look. The traditional Iramian buckskin suit was a novel outfit that the councilman coveted."

"I shall make you one after all is said and done."

"That would be appreciated," Dirk's father admitted.

Before they could face the Hydra, Ken needed to make several torches. He had made some while waiting for Dirk to return, but they could not have too many.

Ken was skilled at all matters to do with survival. Torch making was one such skill. Knowing which trees provided the correct types of sap for burning longest, which wood worked best, and how to fashion the torch itself, these were skills taught to all Iramian boys from an early age.

Ken was ready. Only he worried about fire. Iramians were taught fire making by rubbing sticks together. This method was reliable but took too long. Dirk was pleased to teach his friend something new. Every Alden soldier was furnished a flint for making fire. Ken knew what flint was, his arrowheads and knife were made from it. But what he did not know was that together with a steel knife, it could make a flame appear almost instantaneously.

"You see, my friend," Ken joked, "you *can* teach an old Iramian new tricks." They had a good laugh at that, but now was not the time for foolery, it was time to get serious.

They rode over to the coast where the monster was last seen. Derek went also, to observe his son, but stayed far enough away to not be seen. As if by bidding, the creature arrived. Not as large as Dirk had imagined the creature was still frightening. Ken had learned quickly how to use the flint and steel so had a fire going. He lit all the torches at once. It was time for action.

Dirk attacked the Hydra and had one head off before the monster knew what hit it. Ken went to work rapidly and using a torch had the neck seared closed avoiding the poisonous bites of the remaining heads.

Derek was impressed by his son's valor that day. Dirk and Ken dispatched the hydra, using Ken's idea, in short time. The duo worked well together.

Back at the castle, Dirk and Ken laid the severed Hydra heads at his father's feet.

"Here is the proof you requested," Dirk claimed.

"The proof was in the observation, son. I watched your triumph from afar and I have to admit was overcome with pride."

"Thank you, sir. Whatever the reward, I wish you to give it all to Ken. After all, it was his design, and I could not have done it without him."

"How magnanimous of you, son. But is there not one thing you wish?"

"My life has been changed, Father. I made an oath to do good for good's sake without want of profit."

"I see. Well, son, it behooves me to at least rescind your sentence to the dungeon. I would not want to be responsible for keeping you from doing more good deeds for others."

"Thank you, Father. And now, I wish to see my mother."

Dirk and his mother, looking younger than last they met, had a pleasant reunion this time outside the dungeon cell. Mylyn was so proud of her son. He told her all about his time at Lem and how he felt like a new man. She informed him about Ásil's premonitions which now appeared to be fulfilled.

Dirk and Ken stayed at Alden just long enough for the Iramian to fulfill his promise to Councilman Bin Alden. When Derek donned the buckskin suit, he felt as if he, too, could take on a Hydra.

Mylyn, shaking her head, observed, "When Ken wears the skin suit, he looks striking but, you, husband, look a fool." Fool or not, Derek would continue wearing the outfit in the future whenever he went on a hunt.

It was time for Dirk and Ken to leave. They were both stricken with wanderlust. Their restlessness "itch" needed to be scratched. Derek reminded Ken of the reward his son had refused.

"Sir, my reward is riding side by side with your son. If the reward is monetary, give it to the poor." Which is exactly what Derek did. His son's influence was infectious.

The duo spent Drun, Gofra, and most of Hedra , the 10th, 11th, and 12th months of the Ertah calendar, drifting from town to village throughout Oram in search of good deeds to perform. At the year's end they found themselves in Riverport which would soon host the year-end Wurm Festival.

That, dear reader, is where this tale ends. To read of the further adventures of Dirk and Ken, one must read ...

Adventures in Ertah

Chapter One:
Vitlashuca

The far-flung oasis at Vitlashuca, conveniently located at the half-way point between the cities of Al Cene and Idon, had, over the years, evolved from an isolated, and difficult to find, watering hole, to a regularly used stop-off for travelers between the two cities. Besides the all-important, and scarce, commodity provided by the ever-replenishing spring, some industrious person in the past saw the commercial benefit to anyone hard-working and diligent enough to set up a trading post to provide weary wanderers with any provisions needed for the next leg of their journey.

That industrious person was Ras Q'bar, a roguish fellow from the streets of Al Cene. He had run the operations of this important way- station until his untimely demise at the hands of a jealous rival. His family had taken over operations ever since. Shra Q'bar,

Ras' current heir presumptive, was a sharp-witted businesswoman, and ran Q'bar's Trading Post and Import Emporium with a deft hand. Nothing happens in Vitlashuca that Shra is not informed about.

In addition to running the store, Shra's main duties included overseeing the bazaar, supervising the management of the Caravanserai, or inn, and operating the Jantala, the massage salon, one of her most profitable enterprises. On the mundane side, she must maintain an outfit of guards for the post's protection, see to the upkeep of the birdhouse and warren, their only source of fresh meat, and attend to any, and all, general custodial work needed around the oasis. In other words, she was "the boss."

The Caravanserai, another of Ras' money-making brainstorms, catered to the more discriminating traveler, weary of the routine bivouac of a caravan. The inn was under the care of Thrina Q'bar, Shra's favorite cousin. Although submissive to Shra in all things Vitlashucan, Thrina was a force to be reckoned with when it came to the inn. Hard-fisted, as were all of the Q'bar bloodline, she ran the inn with a firm resolve. She made sure there was a place for everything, and everything was in its place. She knew the whereabouts of all her employees, at all times, including the newest one, a young foundling boy named Po.

The waif, initially begging for scraps in the bazaar, out of necessity, resorted to the age-old process of "snatch and run."

"Stop! Thief!" the merchant man shouted, as the little vagrant made his getaway.

"Somebody stop that imp! Don't let him escape!

Although malnourished, the youth was quick, and avoided most attempts at capture, until a burly guardsman grabbed him by the scruff of his neck, and ingloriously ended the chase.

"Oh no you don't," growled the guard, "Where do you think you're going?"

"I just wanted something to eat," bawled the urchin, "and they have so much. Surely they can spare this." He held out his hand to display a shriveled date.

The guardsman, feeling a little sheepish at having apprehended such a small criminal, looked around for a way out of his predicament. As luck would have it, Amah, an attendant from the inn, came to his rescue.

"I've been looking all over for you," she lied, as she approached the boy. "Shra is going be very mad when she hears about this."

At the mention of Shra's name, the guard immediately transferred the boy into the attendant's hands. No need to upset a Q'bar, he thought.

"Have you got a name, boy?" Amah asked the ragamuffin, when they had gotten a safe distance from the guard.

"Po," he stammered back.

"Well, Po, I'm going to take you back to the inn with me. So be on your best manners, if you have any, that is."

"Yes, ma'am," the child's confidence being bolstered by this promising bit of serendipity.

The entire staff, including the usually dour Thrina, was immediately smitten by the child and fussed over him like a new-born, even though he was of an indiscriminate age, probably a prepubescent teen.

Before long, Po had a permanent home at the inn, and became a regular fixture around the place. He was found to be very useful as a gofer. "Po, gofer this, or Po, gofer that," became a common request during the hustle and bustle of the day. Po had never been happier.

Chapter Two:
Riverport & Beyond

The Rusty Anchor was very busy, what with the Wurm Festival in full stride, along with the usual clientele of gamblers, drinkers, and adventurers, tonight, the pub was "standing room only." Not that Borac, the owner, was complaining, mind you. Business had more than doubled since the beginning of the annual festival five days ago. It was the last night, so he knew business wouldn't be this good for another year.

"Drink up, everyone," bellowed Borac, "'cause tomorrow, it's back to the ol' grind." A low groan could be heard throughout the room at the realization of his words.

Over the din of the crowd could be heard a banging at the door, as if someone were locked out and needed to get in. Following the knocking, an important-looking fellow entered the tavern and all became still, so as to see

"

what, was what. When the man determined he had the attention of all, he began his speech.

"Citizens of Riverport, and any others who are present, please take heed of what I am about to communicate. I am an envoy from The Most Sovereign Sultan of Al Cene, Ifn Adee. It is with solemn brow that I must report to you the most heinous of news – the kidnapping of the Crown Prince's betrothed."

At this news, the room was filled with mumblings, and loud outbursts. For you see, the betrothed spoken of was one of their own. Auria Cara was a 16-year-old maiden, who, not just five days ago, was crowned the queen of the Wurm Festival. Upon her winning the title, she was chosen, by the Sultan, to become his son's bride. This choice was all important to the two city-states of Riverport and Al Cene. For centuries now, the two municipalities had pledged to keep tolerant interrelations, literally, for the sake of the Tunnel.

The Tunnel connects Carfia (at Al Cene) with Pero (at Riverport). Nobody seems to know when the tunnel was constructed, or by whom. Legend tells of how it was created by giant, migrating monstrosities called Wurm, who, like some animals, return to their home soil for spawning. The mammoth beasts are now a myth from by-gone days, extinct, so everyone prays. Upon its discovery by man long ago, the Tunnel has been used as a way of travel between the two continents, as the Perilous Straits make progress by sea nearly impossible.

With the passage of time, humans, and dwarves, have made many improvements to the Tunnel, mostly in terms of reinforcement and size. Two-way transit is now an everyday occurrence, with abundant room for wagons in both directions. With the aim to maintain unrestricted use of the underpass, the two city-states have a long-standing accord to also stay connected genealogically.

"I have been charged by the Sultan," the envoy continued, "to canvass the area and obtain the best of the best to rescue the girl. Anyone with the expertise and courage is summoned to the palace in Al Cene tomorrow before the sun has reached its highest position. May the Almighty M'Olah be with your decisions. Oh, and if I failed to mention it, the Sultan has promised your weight in gold for her safe return."

This "promise" started the mumblings and outbursts to begin anew. Several patrons hurriedly arose and left the establishment to Borac's chagrin.

"Let's toast to the successful return of our Wurm Queen," Borac proposed. But his feeble attempt to keep the taps flowing, was lost in the excitement of the moment. He would have to wait another year for such prosperous times. A soft-spoken curse for the Sultan barely escaped his lips.

"We must be discreet," the young mercenary said in a hushed tone. "There may be others who wish to obstruct our progress if they knew our intention."

"Understood," whispered back his companion, Ken, a native of Iram, whose real name started with "Ken," but then went on for several difficult to say, and remember, syllables.

The gifted soldier, Dirk Bin Alden, with Ken, had just rendered the toll and entered the Tunnel on the way to Al Cene and a midday meeting with a sultan.

"Be observant, my friend," warned the soldier-of-fortune, "for this campaign may be our last, one way, or the other."

The two mounted adventurers disguised themselves as ordinary travelers, not wanting to look in a hurry, and steadily made progress through the great borehole. The way was well-lit by a clever system of oil lamps, judiciously sustained by both cities. Al Cene was responsible for the northern roadway, and Riverport, the southern. The latter looked no busier than usual as the two unceremoniously advanced toward their goal. At their present rate, they would surely be there on time.

Well beyond the half-way point of their journey, they were suddenly overtaken and set upon by three brigands who were unaware of their prey's abilities. In the blink of an eye, the highwaymen were the ones being set upon.

The three robbers were dispatched so quickly, and so inconspicuously, that other sojourners were none the wiser. The whole affair caused barely a hitch to their advancement.

Before long, the end of the Tunnel was in sight, and the sun was just over the horizon. They still had plenty of time to rest before the ordeal of the day began.

The gathering of prospective heroes had begun. The Sultan, with the assistance of his Major Adjutant, set about separating the chaff from the bona fide champions and had assembled two bands, one to search north to the Boreal Sea, the other south to Idon, the Emerald Forest, and beyond, if need be.

Dirk and Ken were chosen to be in the southerly group. Their team also consisted of a tattooed, and very large specimen of a man from the Forgotten Isle of Arandar, and, to Dirk's surprise, the Major Adjutant, responsible for his, and Ken's, selections. Each participant was promised the same reward, which would not put a dent in the sultan's coffers.

The reasoning behind the choice of the Arandarian was quite evident, his size alone, was enough to scare off most assailants. And those grotesque markings on his face completed the picture. But, why the adjutant? His worth was a mystery to both Dirk and Ken, but, if the Sultan wished it, who were they to quibble. He must have some skills the sultan deemed necessary.

Unbeknownst to the two, the adjutant, Afnash D'Brini, was a magic user. His spells would come in handy when nothing else seemed to work. He was also the sultan's spy, sworn to keep an eye on the other three, and report back via a crystal, capable of two-way communication with the bearer of its paired jewel.

The trek to Idon meant traveling through Ul, the vast desert that completely covers the upper half of the continent of Carfia. Thankfully, there was a watering hole and trading post midway on their passage. Aside from much needed food and supplies, perhaps some clues could be found to aid in their quest. Dirk would have plenty of time then to size up the complement of this party, keeping a particular eye on the puzzling saracen.

Chapter Three:
Back at Vitlashuca

Po was becoming educated with everything, and everyone in the enclave. Brundi, the blacksmith, Miki, his pet monkey, Faran, the caretaker of the birdhouse, Arfa, the beekeeper, and the laughable Cherna, "Master" (his title for himself) of the warren, were all becoming familiar faces. Madam Viona, proprietress at the Jantala, a place that filled Po simultaneously with both fear, and wonderment, was only recognized, never approached. But, Po had yet to meet Shra Q'Bar. That major omission was about to be corrected, as Thrina sent the errand-boy to the trading post with a missive.

"Make positive that you put this note into Shra's hands only," Thrina charged. "No one else can be privy to its particulars. Promise me, boy." Po pledged to do as asked, but, wondered what information could be so important.

"And, be on your best behavior, boy. Mistress Shra is my dearest family member, and the most important person at this oasis."

"Yes, ma'am."

Even though a short distance, all the way across the street Po was tempted to look at the message (how the youth wished for the ability to read), but, was ultimately true to his word.

Upon entry into the outpost, Po was amazed at the selection of items that could be purchased there. Q'Bar's Trading Post and Import Emporium had available everything a traveler to this area could possibly want. But, most amazing of all, were the variety of confections on display. Cakes, candies, and something dripping with honey, that Po had never seen before, but immediately coveted.

Apprehensively, Po approached the woman behind the counter, thinking she was "the boss."

"Excuse me ma'am." The words were atremble from his lips. "Would you be Miss Shra?"

"No," the woman spoke sharply, having no time for childish activities. "The woman you seek is in the back. Why?"

"I am supposed to deliver this note to her."

"Give me the note, I will see that she receives it."

"But, I was told to deliver it in person, and to see that no one else handled it." Po's mettle was growing by the second.

"Told by who?"

"By Miss Thrina at the inn."

"Oh", she mocked. "Miss Thrina at the inn."

"Yes, ma'am."

"Well, I'm not going back there and interrupt Shra when she's busy. If you have the will, be my guest." Po's mettle began to wane.

Prepared for the worst, Po slowly went to the back of the store. There was a surprisingly attractive woman sitting behind a desk looking over some papers. Po had experience with the way some people looked and their actual character, so was careful not to offend.

"Yes. boy? How might I help you?" She didn't seem to be the ogress expected. Po advanced a step closer.

"I was sent by Miss Thrina at the inn, to deliver this note to Miss Shra. Would you be Miss Shra?"

"That I would be," sternly replied the boss. "Come here, boy, and let me get a better look at you."

Not wanting to disobey, Po approached more closely to the desk, keeping it safely between them for protection. Slowly, and with a quiver, Po gave her the note. She took it as if this whole sequence was but a bother for her. She opened the note then seriously peered down at the boy.

"So, young man, are you the "Po" I've heard tell of?"

"Oh, no!" Po thought. "She knows of my mischief in the bazaar. "How will I possibly get out of this one?"

"Y-y-yes, ma'am," stuttered Po.

"Well, Master Po, it says here that you have been," she paused for effect, "the hardest worker at the inn, and deserving of a treat." Po couldn't believe it! Instead of the expected bad news, a reward.

"My dear cousin and I have spoken of you often, and yes, I know all about the incident at the bazaar." Po made an audible gulp.

"Now, let's see about that treat." She arose from her desk and proceeded to escort Po to the confections. Without hesitation, Po chose the one dripping of honey. Savoring every delicious bite, Po went back to the inn, beaming with joy.

Chapter Four:
Ul

The trip through Ul started without ceremony. Dirk anticipated a slow and tedious trek. There had been little, to no, conversation among the four so far, so, Dirk took it upon himself to get the ball rolling.

"So, Aranac, how long has it been since you were home?"

"Long time," answered the barbarian.

"Do you ever plan on returning?"

Hanging his head, "Aranac banished," was all he said.

His plans for engaging banter dwindling, Dirk changed course and addressed the adjutant. Maybe Afnash was capable of more than two-word answers.

"Say, Afnash, or, can I call you 'Nash?"

"No, you may not!"

"O-o-o-kay." Dirk felt he was being put in his place.

"What brings you on this expedition? Surely, it's not the reward."

"His sovereign majesty has selected me to accompany you because of my many skills.

"For instance?" Dirk asked.

"For instance," he paused to think, "are any of you proficient in magic?" This response was unexpected and spawned more probing.

"Magic, huh? Like, levitation, or pulling a hare from your turban?" This last remark made the usually unemotional Ken grin.

"If you must know, I am practiced in the wondrous ways of M'Olah, which includes spells of protection and aggression. If, and when, your physical powers become not enough, I will step in and resolve the situation. I have been directed to safeguard this mission."

"Well," thought Dirk, "we don't need a nursemaid." But the disclosure of magic was good to know.

Ken rode along at a slow pace, silently, always aware of his surroundings. Dirk had never met a better scout or ranger. The fighter always felt at ease with Ken around.

Twilight was approaching, it was time to set up camp. If all went well, they should reach the oasis before tomorrow's nightfall. The journey had been uneventful, but that was about to change.

Afnash slipped away to, in his words, "pray to his maker." Actually he was communing with the sultan, by way of the magic crystals.

"No, your excellency, all is as it should be. No traces of the girl, so far." Afnash sounded worried as if his life depended on the successful resolution to the quest. Maybe it did.

"There is nothing to report about the other three, except, the fighter talks too much."

On that final word, "much," the ground next to the adjutant began to rise as if there were a trap door in the desert floor. As it turns out, there was.

"A-i-e-e-e!" Afnash cried as he was being captured by a giant trapdoor spider. The spider began to pull Afnash into its burrow.

On hearing the magician's cry, Ken and Dirk were up, and on the attack. The barbarian was close behind. As the three approached, the beast rose to its fullest height, as it naturally would, to scare off predators. Afnash was still in its clutches. Ken, having had some experience with giant spiders, quickly informed the other two, to try to get the spider on its back.

"It is defenseless, in such a position," informed the Imarian, as he loosed an arrow at the monster's head, barely missing Afnash. On hearing this, the barbarian grabbed one of the spider's hairy legs, and with all his might, flipped the creature onto its back. Dirk, sword in hand, jumped up on its huge thorax to deliver the final blow.

"E-e-e-e-e!" the arachnid cried out in death. Dirk never knew spiders could vocalize.

When they found Afnash, he was completely comatose, or so they thought. Who would blame him. But, when the mage came to, as if from a dream, he explained how he had put himself into a trance.

"I did not want to bring shame upon myself with maidenly wails," Afnash admitted.

"So, you would have just become that monster's food?" Dirk was dumbfounded.

"It is M'Olah's way. All creatures are revered, no matter how unsightly." Dirk just shook his head.

"Okay," Dirk declared, "we've had our fun for the night. Let's turn in." As quickly as they had sprung to action, they were all asleep. All, that is, excepting Ken, who could, unsurprisingly, sleep with one eye open.

Dirk was all abuzz while the party broke camp and couldn't help sticking it to Afnash.

"So, about those magic spells, Afnash, where were they last night?"

"I was taken by surprise," confessed the magus. "I was momentarily caught off guard." Attempting to save face, he added," I will be better prepared, next time."

"Let us hope there will be no 'next time,'" opined Dirk. They were all in agreement.

Dirk laid off with the ribbing of Asnash for the remainder of the trip. He didn't want the magician to get more agitated with him than he already was. You never knew when his "skills" would come in handy.

With the sun sitting on the horizon, the walls of Vitlashuca could be observed in the distance. "Finally," Dirk uttered, hoping for some answers at the watering hole.

Chapter Five:
Strangers Meet

Po was on the way back from the apiary to fetch some honey from

Arfa, when the gofer noticed four strangers entering the oasis from the north gate.

"Shra should be informed," Po thought. By delivering this news first, maybe another honey treat would be a just reward. Po had become a favorite of Shra's since that first meeting. Shra sensed something special about the boy.

Careful not to drop the sweet fluid, Po hurriedly walked back to the emporium. After handing the honey to Tameema, behind the counter, Po went directly to Shra's office in the back, not having to ask permission now.

"Miss Shra," Po reported, "I think you should know. I saw four strangers entering from the north gate."

"Good boy," the boss remarked. She was pleased to know that Po was aware of happenings at the oasis, and his first conviction was to inform her. "This errand boy is becoming quite useful," she had to admit.

"Is this news worth a reward?" Po asked.

"Yes, it is," Shra avowed. "Go tell Tameema to give you your choice of sweets." She could not refuse the boy. Who knew that "the boss" had a soft spot?

Shaking her head, but smiling, Shra needed to seriously compose herself to confront these "guests." They need to know that Shra is the one in charge of all Vitlashucan goings on.

Ken and Aranac were content making camp outside, but Dirk and Afnash wished to partake of the comforts of the caravanserai. A soft bed was far more desirable than the cold, hard ground. As the two drew near to the inn, they spotted a young boy heading the same direction.

"Hey, boy," the fighter addressed Po. "Would you show us to the Caravanserai?"

"Of course, mister," Po, emboldened, sticky treat in hand, guided them to the inn.

Before they gained entrance, they were waylaid by, the fighter had to acknowledge to himself, a very handsome woman. Introducing herself, she made it clear that she was the overseer of the oasis. She would not tolerate any misconduct.

"No, ma'am," Dirk replied graciously, wanting to get on her good side, or, maybe more. "We are just passing through to Idon in search of clues to the kidnapping of a young girl in Al Cene."

"The crown prince's betrothed," added Afnash.

"I can assure you no young girls have passed through here for months. I would know. The only new face around here is your escort, Po, who, you can see, is not a young girl." Acceding this, the two entered the inn.

Thrina welcomed them and inquired of their wishes.

"One room, two beds," the fighter replied.

"I prefer a room for myself!" interjected the mage. After all, he needed to be alone to interface with the sultan.

"Sure, sure," said Dirk, "just trying to save us some expense money."

"The sultan has provided funds enough for our travels."

"Is that so?" Dirk remarked enthusiastically. "Well, then, what's for supper?"

Thrina responded, "You will find we offer the best fare for miles around. A little joke," she begged pardon. "But seriously, our warren and fowl are at your disposal. Po will show you to your rooms. Please, refresh yourselves, and return here for a pleasant meal." At that, Thrina was off to prepare the repast.

Po eagerly showed the two to their separate rooms, wishing to hear of their exploits, and all about this kidnapped maiden. It was as if a bard had come to Vitlashuca with tales of derring-do. Entertainment was not a strength of the oasis.

Po had a feeling that the turbaned one would not be as forthcoming as the other, so, after showing the saracen to his room, the youngster did likewise for the fighter.

"What is your name?" asked Po.

"I am called Dirk by my friends, so, you can call me Dirk." Po liked him instantly.

"Have you had many adventures to tell of?"

"I have had my share of trials," Dirk modestly admitted.

"Tell me of your current quest."

"We have been chosen to search for a poor girl, kidnapped from the palace at Al Cene. There are two more with us, but they favor the familiarity of the outdoors, so they encamped nearby."

"I would love to hear more," confessed Po. "Maybe, after your meal, you will have time to continue, that is, unless you are too tired?"

"At last," Dirk thought, "someone who wants me to talk. Especially, about me."

"Sure, boy, just look for me downstairs, and I'll entertain you with my many triumphs." Dirk liked the sound of that. Po was athrill with anticipation.

The meal consisted of rabbit and squab, roasted on a spit, and to compliment, the best rice dish Dirk had ever eaten.

"This rice is the best I have ever eaten," the fighter confessed.

"You compliment out of hunger," Thrina professed. "Surely, in all of your travels, you have had better."

"Honestly, there must be some secret ingredient that makes it taste so?"

"I will admit to nothing," the innkeeper jested, preserving her secrets.

"Well, if our search should still see us here tomorrow, I will assuredly return for more of this delicious dish."

Afnash ate the same meal but was bemused by Dirk's reaction. The fighter had obviously not supped at Al Cene's finest eating houses. The adjutant was not surprised. Afnash arose and excused himself. He professed the need to retire to his room for prayer.

Thrina, always soliciting for Vitlashucan businesses, invited Dirk to partake of the pleasures of the Jantala.

"A nice massage, and gratifying company, is just what you need."

"Well, that does sound mighty tempting but, truth be told, I had promised your young lad a few accounts of my adventures. Where is the boy?"

"He is bound to be loitering around the kitchen, waiting for any leftovers. I will round him up."

"Po-o-o, our guest is waiting for your presence." As if on cue, Po appeared at the kitchen door, chewing on a squab leg.

"Here I am," answered Po, with a mouthful of roasted bird.

Rolling her eyes, Thrina gestured for the boy to draw near.

"Apparently, you have tormented this man into spending his time for your amusement. He could be enjoying himself at Viona's, but, no-o-o, he has been obligated to entertain you."

"It is no trouble at all," Dirk honestly meant it. Although, he must explore the Jantala before he departed.

The rest of the evening was spent recounting tales of adventure, some real, others imagined. He even included the story of the trapdoor spider attack. Po was spellbound. The youth fantasized about being a hero and saving the day.

"What of your current quest?" Po implored. "Who is this girl that was taken?"

"She was the prince of Al Cene's betrothed, but she was not from that city. She had come from Riverport, where she was the current Wurm Festival queen. I actually had a glimpse of her, too. Upon her selection, they gave her a parade through town. Pretty little thing she was." For some reason, Po blushed at this remark.

"Sounds like you might have had a crush on her," Po teased.

"No way," Dirk confessed, "too young for me, I'm afraid, but you, on the other hand," Dirk teased back.

Po was having a good time bonding with the fighter. A nice change from all the women.

"If you have more stories to tell, I would be very appreciative to hear them tomorrow. I will let you get your rest now."

"This has been as fun for me, as for you. Tomorrow it is." With that, Dirk retired to his room.

The magician had spent the night in conversation with the sultan, relating the day's activities. He left out the spider episode - not his finest hour.

"Perhaps some sign of the girl will reveal itself at this outpost. We will make a thorough search on the morrow, Your Majesty."

"See that you do," demanded the potentate. "And, keep an eye on the other three. The barbarian doesn't seem smart enough to be of trouble, but I don't trust those other two."

"As you wish, sire." The connection was broken.

Ken and Aranac were waiting outside the next morning when Dirk and Afnash exited the inn. To save time, Dirk suggested they split up and each take a section to scour for any traces leading to the girl. Ken would search the traveler's camps, and the barbarian, who might spook some people not acquainted with his kind, should explore the oasis and surrounding area. Afnash volunteered to rummage through the bazaar. That left the central buildings for Dirk. He was hoping to meet up with the comely overseer again, and, of course, a visit to the Jantala.

Upon entering the trading post, Dirk was impressed by the wares to be procured there. He must stop by before leaving Vitlashuca. As he explored, who should he bump into, but Po.

"We meet again, lad," chimed the fighter. "Are you following me?"

"Oh, no, sir. This is my base of operations. I must be near to Miss Shra, in case she needs my services."

"I see," Dirk reflected. "In fact, I have come to pay Miss Shra a visit. Would you take me to her?" Po, seeing some interest there, guided Dirk to Shra's office in the back.

"Miss Shra, you have a visitor. It's Dirk, the famous fighter." Po announced knowingly. Shra arose and approached the two.

"Yes, Dirk, I had forgotten your name (not true)." Dirk, getting a better look at her in the light of day, was now assured of her dark beauty.

"Sorry to bother you, ma'am." Dirk, the fighter of men and monsters, had never felt more nervous. "My colleagues and I have started a thorough search of the area. We will attempt to be as inconspicuous as possible. Be warned that one of our troop is a barbarian from Arandar, the Forgotten Isle, and looks like a monster, but, I assure you, he is harmless, unless provoked. I've seen to it he stays on the outskirts of the oasis so as not to frighten anyone needlessly."

"Thank you for that." Shra was growing more impressed by this fighter. "And you, where will you be 'searching?'"

"I thought I would try the Jantala first," he said sheepishly. "That is the perfect place for a missing girl to be found. What, with the slave trade and purveyors of carnal pleasures, where better to look?"

"I will have you know," Shra asserted, "our girls have been hand-picked by Madame Viona, and are the best money can buy." Self-conscious of what she had implied, she quickly changed the subject. "Would you be needing a guide? I'm sure Po would enjoy the change of pace."

"Oh, please!" begged the youth, "You can tell me more tales while you search."

"Are you sure you can spare him?"

"I think we will get along fine."

Dirk, and his trusty guide, Po, were off to the Jantala.

Being polite, Dirk knocked on the door and was greeted by Madame Viona. An ageless beauty herself, she beckoned him enter, looking over his shoulder at the boy.

"I think it best if you wait outside, boy," she advised. Still frightened by her, and the place, Po was happy to oblige.

"What brings you to our humble establishment, good sir?" quizzed the procuress. "Business, or pleasure?"

"Unfortunately, business. Perhaps later, the latter," he cleverly pledged. "I need to search the premises for a missing girl."

"As you wish, sir." With the ring of a silver bell, the pamperers, in all manner of undress, paraded into the drawing room. It being early morning, most of them were resting from the previous night's frivolities.

Embarrassed, Dirk pretended to look away. But, needless to say, he could not.

"I can also supply boys," she impugned, "if that is your wont." She thought of the youngster outside.

"No, that will not be necessary," Dirk replied, uneasy with the proposal.

"I need just take a quick look around, and I will be on my way." As promised, he hastily glanced into each stall, and satisfied, prepared to depart.

"I am sorry for any inconvenience, ladies. I will now take my leave."

"Now that you have seen all of my wares, I anticipate your return in the near future."

"Of that, you can be assured," he promised. He slowly backed out of the room, just to keep a lasting vision in his mind.

Po, coming up to the fighter, quizzed, "What was it like in there?"

"One day, boy," he said, as if in a dream, "one day you will find out." Po was only left with imaginings, which were extremely vivid.

As like Dirk, the other three came up empty.

"A complete waste of time," Afnash carped.

"We'll see about that, later tonight," the fighter confessed. "Maybe you would care to join me at the Jantala, Afnash. It might do you some good."

"I think not, young fighter. I shall be in my room, praying to M'Olah, a thing I believe might do you some good."

"Have it your way, Afnash," Dirk replied. The magician took leave of this silly man.

The dinner was much like the night before. Dirk helped himself to seconds on the rice, which, he learned was something called "pealoff."

"Peal me off some more of that 'peal-off,'" he good-naturedly crooned. He wasn't only happy for the rice but, was thinking of the night ahead.

Po was nowhere to be found. "Probably in the kitchen," thought Dirk. "It was dinner time, after all." Dirk had delighted the boy for most of the day with his storytelling, while doing his best to hunt for clues. "Maybe he is napping after a long day," he considered. But he doubted that, as the boy seemed tireless. He told himself to make nothing of it and proceeded next door to the house of delights.

As before, he was greeted by Madame Viona, who, again, tinkled her little bell. The "ladies" paraded in, this time fully dressed, if you could call it that. He was introduced to each one individually then solicited to choose one for his companion for the night. He thought this ridiculous. "By choosing one," he reflected," I would break the hearts of the rest." The fighter was full of himself.

In the end, he chose the one that reminded him most of "the girl he left behind." Her name was Tianie, who was quite talented when it came to pampering. Dirk was well attended to for the remainder of the evening, then left the establishment with the widest grin he had ever grinned. He was pleasantly surprised that such a place existed in the middle of Ul.

Tomorrow, they would have to say "goodbye" to Vitlashuca as no traces of the girl were ever found. That included saying a fond farewell to Po, the hero-worshipping gofer, that hung on his every word. Dirk had gotten used to having the boy around.

Po was missing. He had not been seen since the day before, and Dirk had been the last to have seen him.

"This is just not like the boy," whimpered Thrina." He would never miss a meal. He ate like an Ulian boar."

This concerned the fighter because he would have to leave without seeing his little friend.

"When you see him next, be sure to tell him 'the fighter' said farewell."

"I will do just that," the proprietress promised. "And make sure to visit here again if your adventuring should bring you near our neck of the desert."

"On my word of honor," he committed.

"That had been a nice respite to this quest," thought Dirk. Not saying "so long" to Po, though, had been the worst part. He worried for the boy and wished no harm to come to him.

"So, Afnash, how many days to Idon from here?" Dirk probed.

"To my best of recollections, two, possibly three. I have only made this journey one other time in my life, as a young man."

"You have been to Idon? What can we expect?" Dirk was honestly curious.

"First of all, you will see men riding on winged serpents, a very unsettling sight, indeed." Dirk could only imagine. "They are the defenders of the citadel. From on high, they can see for miles in all directions to forewarn of impending attack."

"Attack? Who could attack from way out here in the desert?"

"Wandering marauders make home in Ul. We have been fortunate not to be assaulted by them as yet. Periodically, they have been known to make forays on Idon when the need arises."

"Wandering marauders, you say? Maybe ones with a desire to kidnap young girls?" Dirk surmised.

"I had already thought the same," Afnash admitted. "Best to keep one's eyes open at all times to the possibility of a confrontation."

"Rest easy, my friend. As long as Ken is here, we are safe. He is the best scout I've ever known."

Ken, who has been uncommonly quiet, has felt uneasy since leaving the outpost. "Something is not right," he confided to Dirk.

For the rest of the day, Ken was wary of being watched by someone, or something.

They made camp for the night near a small spring that Ken had discovered just off the beaten track. With large boulders for shelter, it seemed the perfect spot. As the fighter, the barbarian, and the mage set up camp, Ken did his usual scouting around to reassure their well-being.

"Let me go! Let me go!" The shrieks disturbed the solitude of the night.

It was Po. The youngster had been following them all day, keeping far enough behind to save from detection, but not far enough to keep from disconcerting Ken.

"Look what I found," said the tracker.

"Po, what were you thinking?" Dirk sounded truly distraught.

"I just wanted go with you on your quest," The youth responded. "The oasis is never as exciting as the tales you told, and did you not tell me that every knight needs his squire?" Dirk was finding it difficult to stay upset at this boy.

"Yes, but I am no knight, and you are no squire."

"You could train me," Po enthusiastically answered. "You will see. I am a fast learner."

"No, I am afraid not," Dirk reprimanded. "It is back to Vitlashuca with you."

"Wait!" Afnash cried out. "It will cost two days travel to return the child. Whatever trail can be found, will have gone dry. It is too much of a bother. His Majesty will not permit it."

"And just how will 'His Majesty' know?" querried Dirk.

Afnash had to think fast. "As his chosen representative, I will, on his authority, make those decisions that will affect the search for the girl."

"So, what about the boy?"

Dirk could only think of two possibilities. Leave the boy alone in the desert to fend for himself or take him along.

"It seems I have acquired a squire," surrendered Dirk.

"You will see how helpful I can be," Po said excitedly.

"You can start now by collecting firewood for our fire."

"Yes, my liege!" The newly appointed squire hurriedly scrabbled about for kindling and anything combustible.

"I will see to it he earns his keep," Dirk surmised, "just to curry favor with the adjutant."

Afnash's warning of marauders made Dirk overly conscious, particularly now that he had to babysit a child.

"I suggest we take turns keeping watch. I will go first." Dirk volunteered. "Who wishes second shift?" When the sequence was arrived at, Aranac second, Ken third, and Afnash last, they all settled down. Afnash, of course, stole away for his "prayers."

The sultan cared nothing about the boy's addition. "Leave him. Take him. It is no concern of mine. My liaison with the northern group has reported no signs of the girl. They have reached Pellopus and the Boreal Sea. On their return, they will brave the stronghold at Lem to see if the elves can be of any help. I put my faith in you, Afnash. Do not disappoint me."

"A mild threat," Afnash hoped.

Bellies full of dried fruits and flat bread, purchased at the trading post, the party began the next portion of their journey. Po sat on the fighter's steed, behind Dirk, arms around him, not just for balance.

Aranac was bored, so he began chanting something in his native tongue. Ken, a fast study, joined in on the repetitive chorus. To hear this odd duet being sung by these two brought a smile to Po's face. The youngster was very excited to be on a quest.

A very long and monotonous day was followed by a tedious night of setting up camp, firewood gathering, eating, then cleaning up. "I suppose most exciting adventures must have some unexciting times, too," Po thought. "Dirk must have left that out of his stories."

The arid camp, no welcome spring in sight, was also sparsely camouflaged, enabling the travelers to see in all directions. What they saw, started out as a small dust cloud, which, Ken knew, meant they were about to have company. The company turned out to be a band of desert brigands, led by a ruffian calling himself Razooli.

"Greetings, travelers," voiced the vandal, sizing up the opposition. "Here's an odd group," he thought. "Easy plunder for us."

"I am Razooli, Warden of Ul. What brings you to my domain?"

"Just passing through on our way to Idon," Dirk said, a bit too nervously. No reason to give away their true purpose. Just then, the reposing Aranac, became the imposing Aranac, as he arose to his full, enormous stance. Razooli, probably seeing an Arandarian in the flesh for the first time, readied his hand on the hilt of his scimitar.

"Whoa! Whoa!" Dirk called out, holding his hands up. "No need for violence here. Why-y-y-y," thinking of some amicable way out of this predicament, "our friend here, as horrifying as he looks, is as harmless as a desert hare."

"Hmph!" was all Razooli could muster.

"We were just settling down for the night. The journey through the desert can be so tiresome. You are welcome to join us," Dirk fibbed, "and partake of what is left of our meal." Eyeing them suspiciously, Razooli turned and led his gang away.

"Thanks," Dirk said to the barbarian. "I think you made him think twice about any funny business."

"You really think Aranac look horrifying?" he seemed gleeful at the thought.

"I was only trying to save ourselves from any unnecessary difficulties that might deter our progress."

The barbarian contentedly returned to his rest.

Each, in turn, manned their posts for the night. A quick morning meal was had by all. Again, dried fruit and flatbread, washed down with warm water from the waterskins. "Idon, with all of its delights, could not come sooner," thought the mage.

Before the sun climbed to its highest point, Ken, looking agitated, rode in from scouting.

"We must prepare ourselves for what is to come!" he announced. "Find something to cover your faces. Hurry, it will be here soon.

"What will?" asked the fighter.

"A sandstorm, from the east. Lash the boy to yourself for his own safety." Dirk did as he was told. "I will see to the horses,"

Out of nowhere, a huge wall of sand appeared in the distance, pulling at Po. Dirk, reeling the child in, and Afnash hunkered down, using Aranac as a shield from the onslaught. Ken was restraining the mounts, attempting to ready them for the assault.

When it came, the midday sunlight vanished and was replaced by an eerie darkness. Thanks to the barbarian's girth, taking the full brunt of the storm, Dirk, Po, and Afnash were spared from the worst. Ken, placing himself between the steeds, was, for the most part, protected.

Thankfully, the storm was over in a matter of minutes, leaving the party a bit confused, but none the worse for wear. Almost. As hard as he tried, Ken couldn't keep one of the horses from getting spooked and bolting off. Turns out, it was Afnash's mount.

"So sorry, sir. Believe me, I tried to hold on to them as best I could."

The magician appeared humiliated at the thought of sharing a ride with one of them. Po was already with Dirk. That left the barbarian or Ken. "The native from Iram", he judged, "being the lesser of two evils, has acquired a horse mate."

The extra weight on Ken's horse required longer rest periods, more often, which delayed their arrival at Idon an extra day. Their food supplies had been depleted after the night meal. They would enter Idon with empty bellies.

The walls of Idon came into view. Atop the walls were cobra head-shaped sentry posts. From this distance it seemed as if the citadel was moving. It was no mirage. Drawing closer, they discovered the cause for this movement was the foretold winged serpent patrol. Before they could reach the fortress, two of the serpent riders landed in front of them.

"State your business," the first to land demanded.

Afnash, controlling the situation, spoke first. "We are emissaries from his royal highness, Ifn Adee, the Mighty Sultan of Al Cene, on a mission of great urgency." The magician spoke with pronounced authority, hoping to impress the patrolmen. It worked.

"Follow our lead," the second patrolman cried, as they took wing.

"Now," Afnash imagined, feeling important, "with an armed escort, they would make an entrance to the fortress in the style he felt they deserved."

Idon had but one way in, or out, through a gauntlet protected by a portcullis. Two guards, forewarned by the patrolmen, were prepared for them. Eyeing the rarely seen Arandarian, they commanded someone on the other side to raise the gate. Thinking it was taking too long, added to his immense hunger, Aranac walked over to the iron barrier and with one hand jerked it open.

"Aranac hungry," he stated.

The two guards were nonplussed and made room for the rest of the party to pass.

"He does have his ways," observed Dirk.

Once through the gauntlet, they were presented with a feast for the eyes. First, and foremost, was an ornate edifice, presumably the royal palace. Rising skyward, the building was decorated by an excessive amount of cobra sculptures in honor of Aa. An impressive staircase with a long queue of supposed supplicants, rose appropriately to the next level. On either side of the steps, through arched openings, a familiar sound poured out.

"Food," yelped the barbarian, as he charged the opening of the tavern.

"My word, exactly," Dirk added, dismounting with Po.

"I could eat a Borealian bear," piped up Po.

"Wherever did you hear of a Borealian bear? Asked Dirk.

"You must have told me about them in one of your tales." Satisfied with the answer, Dirk and the others followed the Arandarian to a much-needed meal.

Thanks to the sultan's stipend, they were able to fill their bellies. Maybe too full. Po enjoyed the dessert most – fresh figs.

"M-m-m-m," the youngster crooned, downing the last delicacy.

Nizaam, the good-natured tavern keeper, advised them to go to The Tired Serpent Inn on the east side of town. Maazin, his twin sister, would take good care of them. Stables for their horses were conveniently located across from the inn. So, they did. Even Ken and Aranac splurged on the sultan's allowance, each getting their own room.

Dirk and his newly appointed squire roomed together. Po was content sleeping on the fancy divan in the fighter's room.

"There is plenty of room in the bed," Dirk invited, indicating a space next to him.

"It would be improper for a squire to sleep with his superior. It is most unbecoming."

"Have it your way, kid."

Dirk thought the child was taking this business too seriously. "It will be difficult to part ways when we return to Vitlashuca," thought the fighter.

"I am off to the bath house. I smell like a horse's rear end. You could use a little freshening up yourself if you know what I mean." Awkward moment.

"I prefer to bathe alone, if you do not mind."

"And where are you going to do that?" Dirk asked.

"I am confident Miss Maazin can provide for me." Trying to change the subject, "What are you going to do tomorrow?"

"We need to find some trace of the girl or her captors. Maybe I can discover something at the baths. Wish me luck." Dirk left.

The bath house was next to the tavern, adjacent to the pillory Dirk had noticed on his way to the inn. Some sorry soul was being punished for something or other, on display for all to see and berate. Friends or family members, Dirk presumed, cowered nearby to assist him home when his discipling had ended.

Dirk was welcomed to the bath house by an exuberant attendant named Boli Bim.

"I will be your personal servant for the evening, sire," announced Boli. "Like they say, 'Your wish is my command.'"

"Good to hear," the fighter replied. "Maybe you can start by giving me some information."

"Gladly, master, just ask away."

"My companions and I are in search of any information leading to the rescue of an abducted girl from Al Cene."

"Ah, sire, your companions have preceded you to our establishment. Follow me." Boli Bim guided Dirk into the baths proper, where Afnash and Ken were already soaking in a pool together. "Plenty of room for another," Boli encouraged. Dirk undressed and slipped into the reviving waters.

"Where is your shadow?" Afnash inquired.

"You mean Po? I think he is a little too shy, not ready for communal bathing, yet. His loss," commented the fighter. "This feels wonderful! After that sandstorm, I have desert in places desert does not belong . Where's Aranac?"

"He wished to explore the comforts of his bed," Ken said. "He will join us later if he ever wakes up."

Boli Bim returned, bringing towels.

"Good sirs, in response to your query for information, I recommend our local prophetess, Alethia. With the sacred guidance of Aa, she can discern what others cannot. She would be the means to your end."

"How does one obtain audience with this prophetess?" asked Afnash.

"One must first receive consent from Emperor Waliwah."

"Very well, how does one do that?" Afnash was weary of this banter.

"Like anyone else. You must wait your turn in line. The emperor and empress will see you when it is your time." This all seemed very logical to the attendant, but Afnash could not be appeased.

"Royal emissaries sent by the most sovereign Sultan Ifn Adee, should not have to be kept waiting like common peasants!" barked the magician. "There must be some possibility to alleviate this situation."

"There you have me, sire, my knowledge is consumed. Perhaps next morn you could inquire of the palace guard. That is my last suggestion for you."

"Thank you, Boli," said Dirk, "you've been a great help." Afnash could not agree.

"Thank you, sir, I do my best. If there is anything else I can do for any of you, just ask." There being nothing, Boli withdrew.

"The day's events have exhausted me," Afnash admitted, "I will now retire to my room. Good evening, gentlemen." Wrapping himself in a towel, Afnash was gone.

"That is the first civil thing that man has said since we began," noted Ken.

The fighter returned to his room finding Po fast asleep on the small sofa.

The following day showed promise. Maazin prepared a suitable morning meal for her guests. While eating, Dirk and Afnash prepared for the day's events.

"I shall present myself as the sultan's ambassador. Surely that should suffice to get an immediate audience with the emperor."

"If that fails?" Dirk asked.

"We will then have to wait, as the bath house boy suggested. We cannot afford to lose our best chance yet at finding the girl." Afnash sounded desperate.

Po was excited about exploring the marketplace while the grown-ups did their business.

"None of your nonsense. Thrina told me about your adventure in the bazaar. Here, take these coins. They will keep you out of trouble." The fighter gave him a handful of coins, more than Po thought necessary.

"Oh, thank you. If I see something good, I will purchase it for you," the young squire replied in appreciation.

"Just see that you don't make a nuisance of yourself. We need to be on the best of terms with the higher ups around here. This may be our only hope at finding that girl."

"I will be on my best behavior, sire."

"And quit that "sire" stuff. Remember, my friends just call me Dirk."

"Very well," a long pause, "Dirk."

Still being early, many of the merchants were in the process of setting up their wares. One, in particular, caught Po's attention. A robust character displaying a number of gourds of all shapes and sizes. It appeared he could make anything from the dried husk of a squash. Eating utensils, water bottles, ladles, and all sorts of decorative ornaments were to be had.

But, Po thought, the most wonderful of all were the musical instruments. Whistles and flutes, stringed implements, rattles, and percussion of varying types were all available for purchase. The gourd man, always on the look for clientele, noticed Po's interest and beckoned to the youth.

"Come closer, child. Afali does not bite. I can see you like my musical toys. Which do you fancy, a rattle, a drum, or maybe this." Afali held out a small, round gourd with holes punched into it. "It is a wind instrument called a momi." Po was instantly bewitched and began to experiment with various combinations of notes.

"How much?"

"Well, let me see. How much do you have?" Po showed the gourd man the coins. "It is your lucky day, child! You have exactly the right amount." Upon hearing the happy news, Po handed Afali all of the coins. Po spent the remainder of the morning composing little melodies on the new device.

While Po was occupied improvising, Dirk and Afnash were doing their own playing by ear. They left Aranac behind. They would make use of his "talents" only when necessary. Plan A had been a miserable failure as the temple guards were unimpressed by the sultan's title. Afnash was beside himself.

"What an insult!" cried the mage.

"Perhaps the guards need an incentive," suggested Dirk.

"Do you mean a bribe?" Afnash was incredulous.

"Your word, not mine," Dirk asserted. "Hey, it might work."

"How much?"

"As much as it takes so we are spared the wait in line."

"Our funds are not limitless. We still have the journey back to Al Cene," Afnash warned.

With an amount agreed on, the two returned to the palace guards with the inducement. Needless to say, it gained the desired results. The guards escorted Dirk and Afnash, forthwith, to the front of the line. Once in the presence of the Emperor Waliwah and the Empress Lafeeta, Afnash began spinning his tale of the kidnapped maiden.

The emperor was indifferent to the story but, not so the empress. Having been a kidnapped maiden herself, a story for another time, Empress Lafeeta empathized with the girl in question. Afnash, suspecting a supportive ear, continued.

"It has come to our attention that your prophetess, Alethia, with the guidance of Aa, could possibly be of assistance, and we would need your approval to have an audience with her." When Afnash needed to be ingratiating, his true worth become obvious.

The empress, with an admiring eye at the fighter, spoke. "If the emperor has no objections?" He waved his hand in complete apathy. "So be it. First of all one must have the proper offering to approach Alethia – the egg of a winged serpent should do. Proceed to the Emerald Jungle, south of the citadel, to acquire an egg. Return here with egg in hand, and we shall prepare for the audience with our prophetess."

"Yet, another setback," Afnash lamented. He was off to let the sultan in on their progress.

Dirk, a little concerned, searched for Po. He found his squire with the barbarian in his room. Po was serenading Aranac on the momi to the Arandarian's great delight.

"It seems we must have an offering for the prophetess. She requires the egg of a winged serpent, and I've been chosen to get it. You two seem content here. If I'm not back by evening meal, inquire of Afnash for funds. Wish me luck." Dirk departed.

Dirk needed to find someone familiar with winged serpents. He asked Maazin. She informed him that his best bet would be outside the citadel, at the serpent stables.

Once again through the gauntlet, the fighter, on foot, made his way to the serpent stables, in the back of the citadel. He was immediately approached by a wizened individual who introduced himself as Rumahn, the serpent caretaker. Perfect!

"Sir, I am Dirk Bin Alden, an agent from Al Cene, who, it seems, must present the prophetess, Alethia, with an offering of an egg of a winged servant."

"I see. You will not find one around here. All our serpents are male. You must enter the jungle and brave the wrath of a mother serpent. I would not wish to be you, sir." Dirk did not like the sound of that.

"Can you give me any suggestions, I mean, do they nest in trees or are they earthbound roosts?"

"They make their aeries in the trees," the caretaker stated. "The mother will sometimes fly off to feed for a short time in the daylight hours, returning to protect her spawn. That would be the best time to obtain the egg. Beware when they begin to flap their wings very quickly.

They build up energy which they inhale and spew back as lightning. Very unnerving."

"Nice to know," thought Dirk.

"Good luck to you, you will need it. Best enter the jungle now as this is the feeding time for most serpents."

"Thanks, Rumahn, you have been of considerable help." Dirk entered the jungle with much apprehension.

The hardest part of this ordeal, as Dirk discovered, was locating a nest. Purposely well-concealed, the nests were practically invisible.

After about an hour of searching, as serendipity would have it, Dirk noticed a movement in the canopy of the tropical forest. A mother serpent was leaving the nest, presumably to go feed. This was Dirk's chance. He shinnied up the tree as quickly as he could until he was face-to-shell with the eggs. Yes, eggs, there were two. He had his pick, so he took the nearest one.

Dirk placed the egg in his pack and started to descend the tree when mama serpent returned. Trying to keep the tree between him and the irate mother, Dirk clambered down and sought shelter. Using skills taught to him by Ken, the fighter was able to conceal himself from any further molestation. Dirk felt it best to lay still for a while, giving the mother time to settle back down in her nest.

"Might as well take a nap," he thought, "I might be here for some time." As his eyes commenced to close for repose, Dirk heard something. It sounded just like someone cracking their knuckles. He moved cautiously so as not to be detected. The sound was coming from his pack. He carefully opened the bag, and peeked in. The egg was hatching!

Soon, a little serpent head popped out of the shell and directed its attention to Dirk. "Squ-awk," it mewled. "Shush," whispered the fighter. The mother serpent was aroused by the familiar sound. She cried out, wanting to find her lost pup. Dirk was faced with a dilemma – try to make a run for it or face the grieving mother. The former was folly, he could not outrun a winged serpent. So, Dirk readied his longbow for the eventual encounter.

The whimpering whelp was not making this any easier. The more it cried, the easier it was for the mother to find them. Plunging toward them at breakneck speed, Mama serpent was upon Dirk in an instant. Having anticipated the attack, Dirk launched his missile. The direct hit was instantaneously lethal. Dirk, still hearing the youngling's cries, was full of guilt. It was bad enough to snatch the egg, but to kill the mother was unforgiveable. Fortunately for Dirk, one egg remained to offer to the prophetess. But what to do about this whining infant? Its mother was gone for good. "Maybe the caretaker will take care of it," Dirk hoped.

By the time Dirk had returned to the stables, Rumahn had left for the night. "Plenty of time in the morning," thought the fighter, "I will return then."

When Dirk finally set foot in his room at the inn, Po, having been concerned for the fighter's well-being, gave him a big hug. Very unsquire-like.

"Oh, Dirk, I was so worried about you. Were you successful?" As if on cue, the baby serpent, quiet until this moment, began its chirping anew.

"What was that?" asked Po.

Dirk opened his pack and revealed his prize.

"Oh, how cute," squealed Po, sounding less and less like a squire. "Can we keep it?"

"Whoa, boy, this is a wild animal and should be treated as such."

"I've heard they make good pets," Po whined.

"Yes, if you have the time to train them and a silo full of fruit to feed them, they are voracious eaters." Dirk declared.

Po, not convinced, "I will immediately go ask Maazin for any scraps from our evening meal. After all. It is just a baby."

"Well," Dirk thought, "just for tonight. Tomorrow it is Rumahn's concern."

Po hurried back with some dried fruits, a piece of meat and some bread.

"The serpent is not a meat eater, Po," Dirk informed the youngster.

"The meat and bread are for you, Dirk. I am sure you were too busy to think about eating. It is a squire's duty to provide for his champion, is it not?"

"Sure, sure," was all Dirk could think to say.

Po went about feeding the young serpent, gurgling little sounds, like a little girl would. "That boy needs to work on his manliness," Dirk mused. "I don't want a girly squire, after all."

"Do not get too attached to the beast," warned Dirk, "tomorrow it is going to the serpent stables where it belongs." The youth pretended not to hear and continued to dote on the creature. Po played the momi for the beast who seemed to enjoy the sounds. It remained quiet when it heard the instrument. "I guess," Dirk supposed, "one night cannot hurt." The fighter would come to regret this decision.

The following morning could not come soon enough for Dirk. Between the crying of the serpent, followed by the not-so-dulcet intoning of the momi, Dirk got very little sleep. The fighter wondered how early was too early to pay a visit to the serpent stables. The boy and his beast were asleep together on the divan. "How fair the boy looks in slumber," the fighter noticed.

After a filling morning meal, Dirk steeled himself for the struggle that was to come.

"Boy, it is time to go to the stables. Best not be left for later."

"A-w-w-w, do we have to?" Po whimpered. Again, not a manly whimper.

"Yes, boy, and stop your blubbering. A squire does not blubber."

Po, stifling a sniffle, picked up the serpent and followed his liege to the stables.

Rumahn had returned and welcomed the fighter and his squire.

"Show him," Dirk commanded. Po held out the serpent.

"What have we here?" chimed the caretaker. Po handed him the serpent. The beast wailed. Rumahn handed the serpent back to Po. The serpent instantly stopped crying. "It appears the creature has bonded with your squire, sir. Nothing to be done about it now. Once a serpent has formed an attachment to its human, it is for life." Not what Dirk wanted to hear.

"If you try to separate the two, the little one will cry and cry, quit eating and die." Dirk wondered which 'little one' he was speaking of.

"So, what do you suggest?" Dirk wondered.

"To start, your squire needs a pouch for carrying the creature. I think I have a spare you can use." Rumahn opened a big wooden box near the stables, poked around for a bit, and came up with a leather contraption for carrying baby serpents. "This is serpent hide, made from a serpent's wings. The beast should be quite comfortable when placed inside. Now it will only squeal when it is hungry."

"Speaking of that," Dirk said, "I've heard tales they eat constantly."

"Not quite," Rumahn answered. "You will need a substantial amount of fruit, though. The marketplace has all you will need, fresh from our very own farms."

Po was taking this all in when the realization hit.

"Do you mean I get to keep it? For real?" Po was exuberant. Dirk could not say "no" to the child. "Oh, thank you, Dirk." Po squealed. "You are the best master a squire ever had."

Rumahn showed Po how to wear and use the pouch.

"I only have one question," Po implored. "Is it a boy serpent, or a girl serpent? I must give it a proper name."

Rumahn checked. "Child, you are the proud owner of a female serpent."

"It's a girl," Po pronounced. "Will I ever have the chance to ride her as your soldiers do?"

"Do not get ahead of yourself, boy. If, or when that day comes, you will need the expertise of a serpent handler, as myself, to teach you." Dirk was thinking how they would be long gone when that day arrived. Ras' problem, not mine.

"Sir, I have a question for you, what became of the serpent's mother?" Dirk took the caretaker aside, so Po would not hear, and explained the circumstances. "That may be of importance in the animal's life as it grows bigger. We shall see." This news did not concern Dirk.

The time had finally come to make the offering to Alethia. Dirk and Afnash presented themselves to the palace guards as before, and, as before, they required a monetary encouragement to bypass the tedious line, Afnash biting his lip the whole while.

Pleased to see the fighter again, Empress Lafeeta, bade him step forward.

"I presume you have the offering." Dirk held up the egg.

"Very nice. I hope you were not too inconvenienced in its acquisition."

"No, your highness," he lied. No need to concern her of the fate of the mother serpent.

"We will take the offering." The empress motioned an attendant to accept the egg. "Return this evening after nightfall and you will have your audience with Alethia."

The waiting was interminable, especially for Afnash.

"Will the sun never set?" he moaned. "M'Olah spare me."

He had been pacing back and forth ever since he had finished talking with the sultan, who was grateful to hear some good news for a change. The northern party had reported back. The elves at Lem were of no use. They were oblivious to the goings-on at Riverport or Al Cene.

"This prophetess may be our only hope at finding the girl," Ifn Adee admitted. Afnash, thinking only of himself, swallowed hard at the implications.

Dirk knocked on the magician's door. "Come, Afnash, the time is upon us." Afnash was so purposeful in his pacing, he had failed to notice the setting of the sun.

"At last," groaned the mage. "M'Olah be praised. Are the others coming?"

"Ken will meet us downstairs. The other two are having too much fun playing with 'the pet.'" Dirk confessed, "Which, by the way, Po has named Daka, the first initials of our names, to remember us by when we are no longer together." Dirk was a little depressed at that thought, he had come to be quite fond of the boy.

"M'Olah willing, that will be soon.," Afnash prayed.

They met Ken waiting at the foot of the inn's stairs. The usually stoic Iramian was quite animated.

"Ken, you seem overly excited," the fighter noted.

"Ken wishes to leave. Something not right about this place."

Afnash, in his eagerness, hurriedly led the way. This time, upon arrival, they were directly ushered to the Great Hall where they were met by Empress Lafeeta.

"Good evening, gentlemen. I see you are three. Who might this Iramian be?" she asked.

Surprised she had knowledge of such faraway places, Dirk replied, "He is my most trusted friend and confidante. His name is quite impossible to say, so I just call him Ken."

"Welcome, Ken. I think you will find our ceremony is much to your liking. But we must not keep Alethia waiting. Follow me."

Two doors to the east of the throne opened revealing a steep set of stairs. Lafeeta led the three men through the doors and up the steps. Dirk and Ken ascended with no problem. Afnash was a bit winded when he finally made it to the top. A large, round amphitheater with an immense altar lay before them. The entire building appeared to be sculpted from a single huge rock. The room was full of devotees of Aa. The empress ushered them to their seats, front and center, apparently a place of honor.

"You should have a perfect view of the ceremony from this vantage point. Simply wait your turn, as you are not the only petitioners. Alethia will face you and address you by name. No need to raise your voice," she warned, "you will be heard." Lafeeta turned and made her way to the royal box seats at the top of the auditorium.

The ceremony began with music played on pipes, horns and drums, the best Dirk had ever heard. While the music was playing, tall flames flared up around the altar. Dirk and Ken were impressed and wondered how it was accomplished. Afnash, having seen a few ceremonies of his own in Al Cene, was appropriately unimpressed.

A group of acolytes walked into the arena and began to chant. Alethia entered, borne on a sedan chair being carried by four brutes. They reached the foot of the altar, then lowered the chair. One acolyte helped the prophetess out of the sedan then up the steps to the altar. Once there, she turned toward a large statue of a cobra. Aa, assumed Dirk. She intoned a lengthy prayer for her god, to the vexation of Afnash.

She turned toward the assemblage. "Praise to Aa!" The crowd repeated her words. "Praise to Aa!."

"Aa be praised!" "Aa be praised," they echoed back.

"I, Alethia, Prophetess of Aa, have been entreated to come before you and, with the power of Aa, answer your queries, both big and small. No question, or person, is too insignificant for Aa, who sees and understands all."

"Let us hope," Afnash muttered .

As forewarned, they were not the only solicitors that night. Several people were led before the prophetess who listened to and answered their queries. Some answers were met with smiles, others with wails.

Alethia faced the crowd. "Dirk Bin Alden, please stand and present yourself." Dirk did so. "You are a stranger to us, but you have bestowed a proper offering to Aa. I will hear your request."

"Thank you, Alethia, but if you do not mind, I would like to leave the talking to my colleague, Afnash D'Brini of Al Cene."

"Very well. Sir D'Brini, make your request."

Afnash had been waiting for this moment for days. He had been rehearsing over and over. He opened his mouth, then nothing.

"What is wrong?! This is the chance you have been looking forward to!" Nothing. Dirk assumed the magician had something stuck in his throat.

"It appears my partner has been overcome by these proceedings. If you will forgive my lack of practice in public speaking, I will make our plea. We were sent on a quest by the most Honorable Sultan Ifn Adee, of Al Cene, to find a poor, innocent kidnapped girl, the betrothed of his son, Prince Ifn Parse. We have traveled for days, with no clues to follow. It is our wish that you consult your god, who's great wisdom can surely be of aid to our predicament." Dirk thought he had sounded convincing.

"Please give me time to consult with Aa." She turned and prayed to the statue of the cobra. After a long interval she turned back and faced Dirk. "Here are the words of the Almighty Aa. 'The girl you seek is closer than you think. Open your eyes and you will see.'" That was it.

Afnash was frantic. "That is it? That was no clue! How will I explain this to the sultan?" Dirk had to agree with the magician this time. "Was this some kind of punishment for slaying Daka's mother?" he thought. "Listen to him, calling that beast Daka," he scolded himself.

The ceremony was over. The finale was as pompous as the opening. The three adventurers stood as if in a trance. Ken was the first to break the silence. "Now what?" Seemed like a good enough question. They were out of ideas.

Completely deflated, they made their way back to their rooms at the inn.

"I need a drink," Dirk confessed. "Maybe more than one."

Po, sensing his foul mood, piped up, "I take it you did not get any closer to finding the girl?

"Closer, no. Totally confounded, yes." The fighter lamented.

"Too bad," Po consoled. "I suppose that means were heading back to Vitlashuca?" Po sounded distraught.

"Your days as a squire are numbered." The fighter was saddened by the thought.

"You will think of something, you always do." The squire was trying to bolster the fighter. "Maybe you should go get your drink."

"That is the best suggestion I've heard in days."

Afnash connected to the sultan. "Your Excellency, I have upsetting news to report. The so-called prophetess spoke in riddles. Her words made no sense. I fear our search is at an end."

"Relate to me her words. I will do my best to interpret."

"She said 'the girl is closer than we think.' She suggested we 'open our eyes' to see. Nonsense, I tell you!"

"Not so fast, adjutant. Think. Have you encountered any girls on your journey?"

"No, sire. Only the young runaway boy I told you about."

"Ah, yes, I recall. The boy from Vitlashuca."

"Yes, your majesty. A good-for-nothing urchin from the streets, I believe."

"Hmm," the ruler pondered. "I suggest you take a closer look at this 'boy,' adjutant. He may not be as he seems."

"As you say, your majesty." Afnash was incredulous. The sultan broke contact. "Could it be?" he muddled. "Impossible."

While Dirk was wallowing at the tavern, Afnash paid a visit to Po's room. He found Po and the Arandarian playing with the slimy reptile. Po was making noises with that infernal gourd device. "How could anyone call that screeching squash an instrument?" he wondered.

"Boy, I am off to the bath house for a relaxing soak. Care to join me?" The adjutant was being overly oily.

"No, thank you," Po answered. "I am good."

Afnash approached Po and extended a hand as if to persuade the youth physically. Daka flared up immediately and hissed at the mage, protecting her master.

"Down, Daka, down," Po ordered.

"You should train your beast better, young one," Afnash warned. "You would not want to have it destroyed for disobedience." Afnash turned and departed. He would try another scheme.

"I wonder why he is more cross than usual?" Po asked Aranac. Aranac shrugged.

Instead of going for a bath, the magician sought out Dirk at the tavern. He had another plan but needed the fighter on his side. He found Dirk sitting alone at a table and looking very despondent.

"Fighter, I have been looking for you. I wish your help to ease my mind. I know this will sound absurd but, I have been agonizing about this for some time now."

"What is it?" Dirk asked, wanting to be left alone.

"You will think me delirious, sir, but I was pondering the words of the prophetess, 'She is closer than you think.' You remember?"

"Sure, sure. What of it?" Dirk was really getting annoyed with the adjutant.

"Well, sir, what if she is, indeed, right under our noses." Afnash was working to win the fighter's assent for what came next.

"Does it not trouble you that young Po always has an excuse to not join us at the baths?"

"What are you trying to say?" Dirk did not care for the direction this conversation was taking.

"It would help quiet my mind if the boy would prove he is, to be sure, a boy. A simple disrobing in front of us would be all. Then, we can go on with our search. No harm done."

"You really think Po is the girl we have been searching? That would be laughable."

"As you say, sir. But it would be a burden off my mind and so simple to manifest. What say you?" "Anything," Dirk told himself, "to get this whining magician to leave me alone.

When the two men returned to the room, Aranac had already retired for the night. Po gazed at Dirk contemplating what was about to come.

"Po," Dirk started nervously. "You are not going to believe what Afnash has brought to my attention." Po glared at the adjutant with outrage.

"He has come to the presumption that you are not a young man. You are, in fact, a young woman. I know, I know, it sounds preposterous but, all you need do to prove him wrong is disrobe, here, in front of us, right now." Po stood quietly, head bent down, as if ashamed. No words. Large tears began to fall down his/her cheeks.

"That will not be necessary. I confess it is so." Now Dirk was the silent one. Po/Auria ran to Dirk and threw his/her arms around him.

"I have wanted to tell you from the beginning but, I did not want to go back and marry the prince. It was ever so much more fun to play the part of a boy. Since my days in Pellopus, wandering the streets and fending for myself, stealing coins and purses from others, I dreamt of one day becoming an adventurer. When you came along, I thought my dreams come true.

Dirk, still at a loss for words at the unraveling of Po/Auria's tale, finally uttered, "What are we going to do now?"

Afnash, grinning and totally beside himself, wantonly said, "I know exactly what we are going to do now – return to Al Cene victoriously." These words did not comfort the girl. Afnash ran off to give the Sultan the good news.

Dirk put his arm around her and said, "We need to talk. I want to hear the whole story."

"I was kidnapped, as they said, by a group of very incompetent outlaws. In fact, it was Razooli and his gang of thugs. I feared being recognized when he approached our camp in the desert. I think his attention was taken up by Aranac's presence."

"It was easy to escape their bonds with the knife I keep hidden on my body since my days in Pellopus. I pride myself in my ability to move like a ghost when I need to. Their thunderous snoring made it child's play."

"How did you end up at Vitlashuca?" Dirk asked.

"When I escaped from Razooli and his men I followed them from just far enough away as to not be discovered. They were the ones who led me to the oasis."

"I knew enough to disguise myself. I used my knife to cut my hair short and wrapped myself to hide my shape, which is one thing I will not miss. Finding rags to wear was as simple as searching through the offal pits outside the fence."

"Of course, my main concern has been Afnash. After all, he was the one who found me in Riverport and had me transported to Al Cene. When I first saw him outside the inn at Vitlashuca, I was sure my days of freedom were over. I do not think he has suspected for all this time, until now."

"He might still be in a fog if it were not for the prophetess' words. I wonder how she knew?" the fighter pondered.

"By the way, what shall I now call you? Po, or Auria?"

"If you would not mind, I have become fond of Po."

"Po it is" the fighter acceded.

"So, Dirk, what happens now? I will not be the bride of that silly little boy. I would rather run off to the jungle and live my days with Daka by my side. I feel like renaming her Dak if you know what I mean."

"I think I do," Dirk said. "Our biggest problem is going to be convincing Afnash not to take you back. Where did he run off to?"

The mage was contacting the sultan via the magic crystals. "Your Highness, good news! It was as you said. The girl was masquerading as a boy all this time. I have to admit her disguise was quite deceptive."

"Well done, adjutant. How soon can you have her back in Al Cene?"

"If we leave tomorrow, early, and ride straight through with but one respite at the oasis, I say we could be back in one week's time."

"Nonsense, forget the respite and return as soon as possible. My son has waited long enough for his bride."

"As you wish, my lord."

As soon as they broke their connection Afnash was thinking of the reward. His motives were purely monetary. With his weight in gold, he would be second in wealth only to the sultan in all of Al Cene. And perhaps some kind of promotion. He was already the sultan's right-hand man, and the prince was heir to the throne. Maybe a sultanate of his own. It was something to consider.

While the magician was contemplating his future, Dirk and Po were contemplating theirs. "Afnash will never agree to let me go. He fears the wrath of the sultan," Po remarked.

"I will be at your side, and I feel Ken and Aranac will be, also. That is a lot of power behind you, girl." Dirk thought it odd calling Po a girl. He was still bemused by the entire circumstances. "My only concern is Afnash's claims of magic. If he is truly a magic user as he claims all of our strength may not be enough. Magic is scary stuff."

At that moment Afnash returned to the fighter's room. "We will be leaving first thing in the morning. Best get as much sleep as you possibly can. It will be an arduous trip back to Al Cene."

"About that, Afnash, old friend, might there not be another solution to this situation? Po has become our companion," Dirk put forward.

"First of all, old friend, we are not friends. If anything, we are collaborators contracted to provide a service to the sultan. I plan to honor my agreement."

"And what if I say 'no'?" Dirk braved.

"Interesting. You are maybe forgetting the reward back in Al Cene? You could do much with your weight in gold."

This was the first Po had heard of the extent of the reward.

"Dirk, I did not know. That is a lot of gold. You would lose all of it."

"I would have given it to help the poor. I cannot receive monetary rewards for good deeds, it is against my oath."

"Even so, I am not worth it."

"You are to me. My mind is made up. Afnash, if you mean to take Po back to Al Cene, it will be over my dead body. And I am guessing there are two others you will also have to 'convince.'"

The magician was not prepared for this new complication. "I see. It is going to be that way, is it? We shall see what the sultan has to say about this," Afnash threatened.

"You keep implying you are in contact with the sultan. How can that be so? Can he shrink himself and fit in your pocket?"

"Of a sort. Magic is beyond your ken and may one day be your downfall. Beware, my friend."

Dirk felt the understood menace in that last word. He knew they would have a fight on their hands.

Afnash again returned to his room to inform the sultan of the recent events. "Sire, forgive me for interrupting your reverie."

"What is it now, adjutant?" The sultan sounded vexed. "The others of our group have betrayed your will. They are promising to put up a resistance. It seems they have feelings for the child."

"You are the magician, are you not? Surely you can resolve this problem with your ways."

"Yes, sire. It may take more time. I will have to consult the library here in Idon. It is said to be one of the best in all Ertah by fellow magicians. Perhaps I can obtain the help I will need to thwart their plans."

"Do what you must, adjutant. Just do not fail me, or else. . ." The sultan broke the connection with visions of unearthly tortures playing in the magician's head.

The next day, Ken and Aranac were brought up to date on the Po situation. Afnash, fortunately, could not be found. They were hoping he had abandoned any ideas of coming against the three. Four, if you counted Po with Dak, Po's preferred name for her pet serpent, now.

If they had searched the Idon library, they would have found Afnash immersed in magical tomes and manuscripts. He had come into an idea in his sleep that would certainly be the remedy to his predicament. They were three, he did not count the girl, mighty warriors, for sure, especially the beast from Arandar.

Afnash would have need of an ally. Someone with a mighty power to outdo the trio. But a being he, Afnash, could have power over. The situation called for a genie. As a magician, he was able to contact the Elemental Planes where djinn, as they were called, resided. He just needed to learn the correct words to summon such a creature.

He had spent the day perusing and studying to discover the supreme being needed-Bassaam the Magnificent. If what he read was true, this entity, could transport Afnash and the girl straight to Al Cene in the blink of an eye. No need for unnecessary bloodshed.

With Afnash missing, the Party of 4+1 or, the Po4+1, as I shall now call them, decided to make a clean getaway. But, where to? Definitely not back to Al Cene or Riverport. Vitlashuca would be the first place the magician would look. Alden was too far away. So, too, Iram. Aranac was banished from Arandar and sported the mark of shame.

The only place that seemed logical was the jungle. Afnash was not familiar with the region. The overhanging trees and vines would provide concealment. Ken was an expert at covering their trail in case they were being followed. And there would be plenty of fruit for the rapidly growing serpent.

"I forgot to ask Rumahn how quickly these creatures grew."

"Dak is not a creature," Po pouted, sounding more like the girl she was, Dirk noticed. "She is our friend."

"Sorry, miss," Dirk accentuated "miss" to get a rise out the girl.

"Ooh, sometimes you can be so infuriating," insisted Po.

Do you know how difficult it is to be sneaky when you are as big as an Arandarian? It made Ken's job of concealing the trail that much harder. They left their mounts back in Idon. They would never make it in the jungle. This made their getaway slower, but less detectable.

This jungle reminded Aranac of home and his trial with the huge snake during his Ceremony of Courage. That, in turn, made him think of Amarac. He wondered how she was and about all his adventures he would never get to tell her.

It also made him think of Clac. He hoped she had made a home for herself in Salé. He wondered how far they were from the west coast of this landmass. Maybe they could escape on a ship. The angry man would never find them then.

"Dirk," he had never called him by name before. "How far to west coast?" He had also never asked him a question before.

"Why do you ask?" Dirk was enjoying this first-time conversation with the Arandarian. "Aranac know sailors on ship. We could escape the angry man if we were on a ship." It seemed logical to the man-beast.

"Good to know, Aranac. You must tell me more about your life sometime, it sounds very exciting."

Dirk may not have been a whiz at calculations in school, but he was in history and geography. He had studied all known maps of Ertah and was confident in his knowledge. He estimated it would be a day's hike, maybe two, to reach the sea on the west coast of Carfia. At least it was a destination to somewhere instead of away from.

They all agreed it was preferrable and began stocking up on fruit to last them the trip. Aranac felt good about his contribution to the effort and hopefully seeing Clac again. When they had all the fruit they could carry, they made a right turn and headed west.

Afnash needed a proper receptacle for Bassaam the Magnificent to inhabit while in the Material Plane. The magician visited the marketplace to find such a vessel. He spotted a very ornate urn that would be perfect. The urn was decorated with what looked like gems but were actually stained glass. At first glance no one would guess the urn was really made from a gourd.

"Good sir, I see are interested in my decorative urn. Be assured all of Afali's wares are of the best quality. Shall I wrap it for you?"

"No, thank you. Afnash was in a hurry. "How much?"

"For a fine gentleman such as yourself a mere pittance."

Afnash thought this man talked as much as the fighter. He agreed to the price, which he really thought excessive, just to be done with the man and continue with his plan. He returned to his room, locked the door, and began his summoning of the djinn.

Nothing happened. Afnash assumed, erroneously, that he must have left something out of the summons or perhaps mispronounced a word. Then suddenly the urn started to turn, slowly at first, then picking up speed. When the magician supposed it could not spin any faster it suddenly stopped, and a fine mist commenced to rise out of the container. The mist grew larger and larger and began to solidify until a red, horned creature appeared before the mage.

"Why have you awakened me?" growled the djinn.

"Many pardons, your magnificence." Afnash had never been so frightened, not even when the giant spider possessed him.

"I, Afnash D'Brini, mage to His Holy Sovereign, the Sultan of Al Cene, have summoned you forth to be of aid in my pursuit of justice. The sultan's son, the prince Ifn Parse, has lost his betrothed. I have finally found her but am being obstructed from returning her to her rightful place by three good-for-nothing thugs." It may not all be true but, hey, he is dealing with a djinn.

"I care nothing about your insignificant amorous intrigues. I was in the middle of a thousand-years-long dream when you dared awaken me." The red creature began to get redder. "Why should I do your bidding?"

"I believe you must provide to me three wishes before you are allowed to return to your plane of existence. The sooner those wishes are granted, the sooner you can return to your dreaming."

"So be it, mortal. Be quick with your wishing."

"I seem to have lost the girl again, so I wish for you to find her."

"Your wish... Oh, I am sure you know the old saying. It is done, I have found her."

"So, where is she?" Afnash said, gnashing his teeth.

"Do you wish to know where she is?" Afnash thought this a trick question. If he says yes, he loses another wish.

At this rate, he would lose all his chances to obtain the girl and his dreams of wealth and power.

"Wait! Do you take me for a fool? I wish for us to be where she is." Afnash thought himself the clever one. In a heartbeat he was in the desert between the jungle and the coast. The djinn was beside him issuing from the urn.

Po4+1 was shocked when the magician appeared seemingly from out of nowhere.

"Greetings all," Afnash said wickedly. "I do hope you have had a nice walk. May I introduce you to Bassaam the Magnificent, my personal djinn."

When the two popped into existence a strange feeling came over Dirk. He started to glow like he had at Lem. The emanation grew until it towered over the assemblage. Everyone, including Dirk, stood in awe of the presence.

"What is this?" shouted the djinn. "Is this a trap, magician? You summon me to your plane to have me face my one true adversary? The immortal Ambassador of all that is Good is like water to my fire. You shall pay for this transgression, puny human."

Bassaam, scanning the area for something appropriate, made a small gesture with his hand and Afnash began to vaporize. What the djinn had found was Po's momi. Afnash completely evaporated and was sucked into the hollow instrument.

"You have erred in judgement, mortal. You will remain trapped in the gourd until the correct pitches are found to release you. Then you will be at the bidding of the person responsible for blowing those tones. This curse will last for as long as the slumber you awoke me from. Bassaam has spoken. So be it." With that, Bassaam dematerialized.

The Ambassador of all that is Good returned into Dirk's body.

"Dirk, did you know you could do that?" Po asked.

"Ken says he saw me glowing once but, I had no idea, then, or now, what it all means."

"Do you really think Afnash is inside my momi? Po put the instrument to her mouth and blew. "I do not think he ever liked the sound this made. Poor Afnash. I wonder how long he must be imprisoned in here?" As she said the words, she shook the gourd instrument but heard nothing rattling inside.

"I believe with the magician gone," Dirk remarked, "we have options to make. I would like to hear from each of you on what you would like to do now."

Po spoke first. I would like to go back to Vitlashuca for a visit. Shra and Thrina will be surprised to see me now. Then I would like to go to Idon and take flying lessons from Rumahn."

Dirk would also like to revisit the oasis. Another call at the Jantala and Tianie would feel good right about now. Also, the attractive overseer at the trading post. He would like to get to know her better.

"What about you, Aranac?" Dirk asked.

"Aranac wants to continue to the coast and find pet chicken, Clac." Dirk let that remark slide without a query.

"So, I guess this is goodbye, Aranac. I have a feeling we are destined to meet again. I hope so. Until then, do not do anything I would not do."

There were hugs all around, even from the stoic Ken. He had become fond of the big guy. Aranac received a portion of the fruit for his journey, turned, and took off before anyone could see him cry.

Po4+1 was now Po3+1. Idon was now their destination. By skirting the jungle, they would make better time but still be close enough to a food source. Without the sense of urgency, the progress was less hectic. Ken could scout ahead instead of bringing up the rear. Po spent her time walking trying out little melodies to free Afnash from his prison. Dak slept soundly in the pouch that was getting smaller and smaller for her every day.

"There must be a never-ending number of note combinations. How will I ever find the correct ones?" Po was getting frustrated.

"Keep at it," Dirk said. "Just think, you should be driving Afnash out of his mind by now." To be sure, the magician wanted her to find the tune more than anyone.

As soon as they made it back to Idon they returned to their rooms for a much-needed rest. But first, Dirk went to Afnash's room to see what the magician might have left behind. Oddly, the mage's purse sat on his bed. Hoping to find a cache of coins, instead the fighter found a crystal of unknown variety. He replaced the stone in the purse then placed the purse in his pack. "It might be worth something," he thought.

Back in his room, Dirk realized he was sharing it with a young woman.

"I think maybe you should spend the night in the magician's room." Dirk said awkwardly.

"Why, I remember it was not too long ago you invited me to share your bed," Po boldly said. She enjoyed embarrassing the fighter.

"That was then, this is now," Dirk explained, trying to sound paternal. "Just what I do not need," the fighter told himself, "an adolescent girl wanting to share my bed."

"I think I would prefer Aranac's room. Afnash still disgusts me." She gathered her belongings, including Dak, and haughtily departed the room.

The following morning, they met in Dirk's room to make plans.

"Before we leave for the oasis, I think it would be wise to fill our stomachs as much as possible. There will be no food until Vitlashuca. The sultan's funds vanished with Afnash and I only have enough for our morning meal."

"We also need to retrieve our mounts. With the magician absent, Po, you will have your own horse to ride," Dirk observed.

"And I would like to visit Rumahn to see if he has any bigger carrying pouches. Dak is growing so quickly. I have a few more questions to ask him about the b . . ." he almost said "beast" again, "about flying serpents." Po looked at Dirk guardedly.

After the meal was eaten and the horses were retrieved, they made their way behind the citadel's wall to the serpent stables. Rumahn was pleased to see them but, especially, to see how the serpent was prospering.

"I was wondering if you could provide us with a bigger pouch for the animal. It is outgrowing the one we have."

"Sure. Sure. Wait just a minute." He rummaged through the same box as before and came up with a larger pouch. "If you do not mind, I will trade you for the smaller one." They made the exchange then Dirk continued with his questions.

"Rumahn, I have a few questions to ask about Dak."

"Dak?"

"Yes, that is the name Po has given the animal."

"I see."

"First of all, how soon will it be too big to carry in the pouch?"

"Each serpent is different, of course, but on average I would say Dak will be big enough to fly in a month or two."

"That soon? Is flight something they just know how to do or, do they need to be taught?"

"The mother is the one to teach her young. But seeing how this one's mother is no longer with us, makes learning to fly more difficult. I am not saying it would be impossible, just more difficult. I will be available when that day comes."

"Thank you, Rumahn. I have no way of telling where she or I will be when that day comes but, I will keep you in mind."

"As you will, sir."

With no one sharing a mount, Po3+1 made good time on the trail. Ken was vigilant in keeping an eye out for Razooli's gang or any other now that Anarac was not with them for reinforcement. Po had been quiet for most of the trip except for her tooting on the momi. Dirk wondered how Afnash was faring with all the incessant piping.

Ken, being the skilled ranger he was, scrounged up some food. Large, red fruit from some desert succulent was better than nothing.

Dirk took this break from the journey to re-examine the crystal he had found in the mage's room. He held it up to the campfire to get a better look. He asked Ken if he had ever seen such a stone, which he had not. Suddenly, the rock began to speak.

"Adjutant, are you there? What has been happening?" Dirk stared at the stone in wonder

"Hello?" Dirk said to the rock. "Who is this?"

"I am Ifn Adee, Sultan of Al Cene. "And who are you?

"I am Dirk Bin Alden, and I have some very bad news for you. Your adjutant, Afnash, has been imprisoned in a gourd by a djinn and we cannot get him out."

"A gourd you say?" the sultan almost chuckled. "That is neither here nor there. What about the girl? He told me you had been traveling with her for days. I want her returned as soon as possible."

"Well, sultan, I am afraid that is not going to happen. You see, after hearing her side of the story we all feel she has the right to choose her own path. Being your son's play toy is not one of those choices. There are numerous females in Riverport, some would even be willing, that would jump at the chance to be the prince's betrothed. I suggest you look there again."

"This is outrageous!" the crystal shouted at Dirk. It somehow did not have the effect the sultan desired. "You and your friends have not heard the last of this!"

"We will see about that." uttered the fighter. Dirk put the crystal in the purse, dug a deep hole, and buried both.

The trip continued without mishap, and they reached the oasis by nightfall of the following day. Before walking in on Shra or Thrina, Dirk had been planning what to do on their return. His first stop was not at the inn or the trading post but to the Jantala.

The ladies there were specialists at making a woman look her best. Dirk wanted to give something to Po as a memento and thought the transformation from urchin boy to the pretty girl he remembered from the Wurm Queen parade the best he could do.

They set up camp at the traveler's camp closest to the Jantala. Po made sure Dak was safe and secure. All three crept over to the establishment not wanting to be seen by anyone that might recognize them. Dirk lightly rapped on the door. Viona opened the door smiling when she realized who it was.

"Dirk, you have returned. Come in, come in. And you have brought friends this time." Dirk explained to Viona the reason for their visit.

"Are you not the clever little one," Viona said to Po. 'When we have finished with you, your own mother will not realize it is you."

That remark stung a little. Po wished her mother was still here to see this. While the ladies went to work Dirk and Ken, yes, my friend, even Ken could appreciate some female pampering every once in a while, partook of the Jantala's amusements.

The time for the presentation had arrived. The ladies marched Po into the room with much pageantry. At first Dirk was not sure which lady was which. When he comprehended the reality, he was dumbstruck. Ken used a finger to close Dirk's gaping mouth.

She was more lovely than he remembered from that night in Riverport that seemed so many years ago.

Ken actually spoke first. "You are a girl, Po. And a pretty one."

"Thank you, Ken." She felt a little silly saying that. "And what do you think, Dirk?"

The fighter was still speechless. He cleared his throat. "Not bad, for a street urchin," he joked. Po was not amused, and he knew it. "I am just kidding. You look absolutely beautiful, Po." And he meant it.

"Now for the unveiling next door and across the road."

Dirk and Ken entered the inn, keeping Po well-hidden behind them.

"Dirk, welcome back to Vitlashuca. Introduce me to your friends." She had noticed a smaller person in the back.

"Thrina, this is my best friend, Ken. Ken, Thrina Q'Bar."

"Likewise, welcome," the proprietess said. "You must be very fortunate to have a friend such as Dirk." And the little lady?"

"Do you not know me, Thrina? I am Po." Thrina looked puzzled.

"Is this some kind of joke?" The inn keeper was astounded.

"No joke, Thrina. I am, and always was, a girl. I disguised myself as a boy to avoid capture." With Thrina still reeling with questions they all went across the road to surprise Shra.

Tameema was manning the counter and with fingers to lips Thrina cautioned her to be silent. Thrina called to the back office, "Shra, come and see who has returned to our home." Shra walked out from the back and, upon seeing Dirk, walked up to the fighter and gave him a very un-Shra-like hug.

"Welcome back, Dirk Bin Alden. How goes your search for the missing girl?"

"We have located her, and she is here with us now." Dirk stepped back so Shra could see the girl.

"And such a lovely girl she is. It is no wonder the sultan wants her returned. It is funny, though, she looks familiar to me."

"Her name is Auria Cara but, you knew her better as Po."

"Po? Our little beggar boy, Po? I do not believe it!"

"Believe it, Shra," Po said.

Dirk added, "So what do you think of your little gofer now? The ladies at the Jantala have done a marvelous job."

"Oh? You visited the Jantala before coming to see me?" Dirk could not tell if she was hurt or just kidding.

The Po3+1 moved into the Caravanserai for the remainder of their visit. Dirk enjoyed getting to know Shra better, and she likewise. They had much in common but, foremost was their fondness for Po.

Po was enjoying being a girl again. She visited the Jantala as much as possible for all the lessons she missed out on growing up motherless. Dirk felt she was spending too much time there, but she seemed to enjoy it so.

"What can it hurt?" Shra asked. "She has been living her life as a boy with men like you, she needs some girl time."

"I suppose so," Dirk admitted. And that was that.

As all good things must end, it was time to return to Idon for flying lessons, both for Dak and eventually for Po. Dirk and Ken, with nothing better to do, would join along for the ride. This got Dirk thinking about the future.

"Who has the responsibility for Po?" he wondered. "She is not my child, so why do I feel as a parent would?

Can I merely leave her to fend for herself in Idon? He felt his abilities would be required elsewhere. He was too young to settle down in one place and raise a child." He felt trapped.

On the night before they were to leave, a fortunate thing happened. While noodling on her momi, it began to vibrate. "It had never done this before," she said to herself. "I wonder . . .?" Her thoughts were answered when a mist appeared from the gourd and materialized as the adjutant, Afnash.

"Salutations, miss. I, Afnash D'Brini, am at your service. And by the by, thank you for releasing me from that tedious cell. There is not even a pillow to comfort myself."

"How is it being a djinn?" Po inquired. "I do not know. I have not had the opportunity to try. Now that you have discovered the correct pitches, I hope to see the outside more often."

"Oh, the right notes! I hope I can remember what they were. I was just playing around with the momi."

"Think, girl!" the djinn was totally annoyed with this child.

"I know I am going to regret this but, send me back to the gourd and try again. And this time remember."

Po wished him back in the momi and blew the notes she thought she had played. Nothing happened. She tried again. Likewise, nothing. As the ancient proverb says, it is the third time that is successful. And so, it was.

"Oh, good. Now please write them down somehow so you will not forget them." Writing not being her strongpoint, she used her knife to carve a picture on the wooden floorboards of which holes to open and close.

"Now, as I have said before, I am at your service. Do you wish something?" Po really did not need anything at the moment, but wanted to test this out.

"There are confections in the trading post dripping with honey. I wish to have a plate of them on the table by the bed." She hoped that was clear enough.

"Very well." With a big flourish from the djinn, it was so.

"Anything else, miss?"

"No, that will be all. Except," she stopped short of wishing him back to the momi, "in appreciation, I would like you to have this." She handed Afnash a large pillow from her bed.

"You are too kind, miss." With those words, he vaporized into the gourd.

The next morning, Po went to Dirk's room, knocking on the door first.

"You may enter, whomever you are," the fighter announced.

"I it is just me, Po." The girl seemed giddy. "Actually, I have brought someone with me." She played the four notes and waited for the fun. Afnash appeared as before.

"Do you wish something, miss?"

Dirk, seemingly glad to see the adjutant, "Afnash, old friend. How is it with you?" The fighter did a terrible job of disguising the humor in his voice.

"As you can see, I am in the service of Miss Cara." The djinn was trying his best to be the adult in the situation. "So, I ask again, is there anything you wish?"

"Not at the moment but, stay close, for I feel we will have use of you this day."

"Surely, you jest, miss. Where else could I be?"

"Sorry, Afnash. You may take your leave."

"As you wish, miss." Again, he disappeared into the momi.

"Well, that was interesting," Dirk stated. "What do you suppose he does in there all day?"

"I am not sure but, I am sure it is lonely."

"You will not get me to feel sorry for the man. Remember who and what he was."

"I know," Po whined. "But maybe I can bring him out of the momi more often, just to breath fresh air."

"Be careful when and where you make him appear. There are many unscrupulous people who would love to have their own personal djinn. I hate to say this but, he may be the answer to my worries about your safekeeping."

"Why, Dirk, you worry about me?" Po said, being the coquette.

Dirk now knew the girl was spending too much time at the Jantala. The sooner they left Vitlashuca, the better.

"I am concerned for your well-being in Idon when Ken and I leave you." Dirk was trying not to be playful at this serious moment.

"Oh, you will be moving on?" She did not want to think on that day.

"Ken and I are not the types to settle down. I am sworn to use my abilities whenever, and wherever they are needed. "

"Oh, I see." Po did not want to cry in front of the fighter.

"That is why I am glad to see you now have Afnash to take of your every need. Besides, you will be so busy with your flying lessons there will be no time for me or Ken."

"It is not Ken I will miss so much." Her lower lip protruded. "Oh, Dirk, what am I to do without you beside me." The tears were finally flowing.

Dirk put his hands on her shoulders. "Listen, Po, whenever you want to see me, just ask Afnash and I will be at your side."

"Promise?" She sniffled.

"I do not think I will have a say in it." Po chuckled. "Just do not make it an everyday habit." Po could not hold back. They fell into each other's arms and stayed that way for a long while.

They made all their farewells and proceeded to depart as usual. When they reached a fair distance from the oasis, they stopped. Po summoned Afnash. This would truly be a test of his new powers. She wished for their entire party to be transported to the road outside Idon, far enough to not be spotted by the flying guards. As if it were the easiest of undertakings, the djinn waved his hand, and it was done.

"I think you are liking this too much, adjutant," Dirk commented. "This was meant to be a punishment, after all." They all saw the irony. All, save for Afnash who was attempting to make the best of a terrible curse.

"The fighter has turned into the jester," Afnash said cheerlessly.

Po returned him to the gourd, and they made their way to Idon. Maazin, surprised at her transformation, hired Po, and gave her room and board for doing work around the inn. The innkeeper told Po when she was older, she could work at her brother's tavern where the tips would be flowing for such a pretty girl.

Po and Dirk returned to the serpent stables where Rumahn set up a space for Dak. The serpent was nearly ready to be taught how to fly. Po would return daily to spend time with her pet.

Now, dear reader, the time has come to finish the present tale. Po is situated to Dirk's liking. He and Ken will take leave for future exploits. If you have enjoyed these tales as much as I have enjoyed telling them, perhaps you will read my next volume . . .

The Further Adventures in Ertah

Appendix 1.

Ertah Common Calendar

365 days in a year

12 30-day months

5-day Festival to make up missing 5 days / 6th day every

4 years

Festival Days : 1st day – 5th Day

Bonus Day (Every fourth year) – Wurmday

Months (5 Weeks x 6 Days)

Days:

Sunday	Months: Rog	Bron
Moonsday	Frin	Algus
Tinsday	Obuck	Cadra
Veltasday	Sely	Drun
Thronsday	Min	Gofra
Fradensday	Juf	Hedra

www.ingramcontent.com/pod-product-compliance
Lightning Source LLC
Chambersburg PA
CBHW021549310726
48972CB00003B/752